THE AMERICAN DIAMOND

An Ainsley Walker Gemstone Travel Mystery

J.A. JERNAY

PLOTWORKS PUBLISHING

ISBN (electronic): 978-1-960936-41-7

ISBN (print): 978-1-960936-42-4

CHAPTER ONE

As the psychiatrist looked over her case file, Ainsley Walker mentally plotted her escape.

She was sitting on the edge of the leather couch in his office, above average height, hands folded in her lap, her multicolored boots crossed demurely at the ankle. She'd worn her street clothes all week, the nurses' requests be damned.

The door was only two meters away, and the admitting station was only a few more beyond that. She could make it in less than four seconds. Ainsley had been a high school track star, all-state in the 50-meter, 100-meter, and long jump. That had been over ten years ago, but she knew that she still had those quicks.

Her attention returned to the psychiatrist. He was pinching his nose between his thumb and forefinger as he flipped a page, totally engrossed in her file. She felt a twinge of excitement at seeing a man take this much interest in her. Quickly she realized how pathetic those feelings were.

"Would you say that you feel better than you did when you entered this institution?" he asked.

Ainsley Walker knew that she needed to play for points.

Tell them the things he wanted to hear. Show him the results he wanted to see. Here, deep in the bowels of a psych ward, there was no other way.

"Absolutely," she said.

"You have been refusing all medication," he said.

"True."

"Then why did you ask to come here?"

The female psychiatrist who'd admitted her already knew the answer to that question, but she'd already left on a two-week vacation. Ainsley's eyes roved this guy's bookshelves, his family photos, searching for the right answer.

"I just needed a break. It was all too much."

The psychiatrist nodded hard. His eyes scanned the file. "You're married?"

"That's complicated."

He looked at her over his spectacles. "I'm listening."

"You want the short version?" He nodded. Ainsley drew in her breath. "I supported him through law school. Then he left me. I don't know where he went."

The psychiatrist nodded again. Ainsley was getting tired of that. "Do you have children?" he asked.

"No."

"Any family in the area?"

"No."

"Tell me why you think you should go home today."

"Because I'm ready to face my life again."

He made a note but his face betrayed nothing. She decided to hazard a joke: "And I want to look at some paintings that haven't been caulked to the wall for my protection."

The psychiatrist smirked. When he finished writing, he slid the pen in his shirt pocket and removed his glasses. "Ainsley, you are in no way clinically depressed. Temporarily depressed, yes. Do you mind if I ask you another question?"

"Sure."

"You do mind?"

"Whatever," she said, "just ask."

"What would you say is your biggest problem?"

She knew the answer, but it stuck in her throat. "I ... don't have a purpose." She felt more words spilling out. "All my friends are having kids, I don't see any kids in my future."

"What about your work?"

"All I've had is a series of jobs. I don't have a career, or a calling, or anything meaningful."

He nodded. Ainsley wanted to reach over the desk and smack him. It felt so condescending after she'd just emptied her heart.

"So how are you going to address these issues?"

She shrugged. "If I knew that answer, I wouldn't have checked into this happy hotel."

The psychiatrist shut the folder. "I'm going to discharge you. You may gather your personal belongings from your room." He looked over the top of his glasses. "And, as a fellow wanderer, I wish you luck."

Ainsley stood up, feeling both relieved and nervous. She paused at the door. "You know, while you were looking at my folder, I was planning an escape."

"It wouldn't have been the first time," he replied. "But you were leaving today anyways."

"Why?"

"Your insurance only pays for a week."

CHAPTER TWO

Outside the facility, Ainsley waited on the concrete steps for her ride. Above her, in the branches of a stately oak, a bird tweeted an empty melody.

Nothing tweeted back. Ainsley wondered if the bird had been abandoned by its mate.

She applied some lipstick in her compact. It felt good to pretty herself up. The simple stuff was important.

Slung under her shoulder was another thing that made her feel better about life: her white bag. It had killer hardware, good details, both sass and class. She'd found it at a semi-annual sale years ago, hidden at the bottom of a bin of ugly castoffs. Ainsley had become convinced that it had been waiting for her all along, like the perfect kitten at the rescue.

A gray sedan pulled up to the curb. In the back was an empty baby seat. In the driver's seat was her friend Deirdre.

She left the engine running while she came around the car for a hug. "Oh Ainsley," she said. "My God, what happened? You lost so much weight!"

"It's the eight-week miracle diet," replied Ainsley.

"Just remove husband, right?"

"Deirdre, I'm a walking skeleton," she said.

Her friend checked her watch. "We have to hurry. Justin is being fussy and Marguerite has to leave at two o'clock."

As they drove onto the freeway, Ainsley noticed that Deirdre's shape had changed too. Ainsley remembered her friend's tight skirts that had earned both of them free drinks when they used to go out to nightclubs. That had been less than four years ago. Those days were gone now. Since then, Deirdre had traded the fishnets and heels for sweats and pacifiers.

"Toddlers are *such* a pain," Deirdre said. "Strike me down now for all the shit I used to say about full-time moms not having real jobs."

"Not enough lightning bolts in the sky."

"It's like this constant state of medium-level attention," Deirdre said. "Seventeen hours a day. It's just *exhausting*." She took a drag from her cigarette, then lifted it back to the ribbon of air at the top of the window. "Matt would kill me if he saw me doing this, but sometimes nicotine just mellows me out." She looked over at Ainsley. "So what's up with *you*? Feel any better?"

"Yeah. I was protected from the evils of dental floss."

"Good," said Deirdre. "Oh, I have news for you." She paused dramatically. "I saw his car."

Ainsley closed her eyes. There it was. In less than five minutes. Why did people keep *talking* about him? In her mind, that asshole was as good as dead and buried. But everyone she knew insisted on digging up his metaphorical remains with a potato spade, turning them over, poking at them, discussing them.

For her part, Ainsley just wanted to get away. Start life over.

"Whose car?" she said.

"Don't play dumb," said Deirdre. "*His* car."

"Did you smash it?"

"It slipped my mind," she said. "There was a screaming kid throwing rattles at the back of my head."

They were cruising down Ainsley's street now. Deirdre slowed the car down and craned her neck. "You know what, I forgot which one's yours."

True, it was lined with identical gray apartment buildings, Soviet-bloc style...but still. "Has it really been that long since we hung out?" said Ainsley.

Deirdre looked guilty. "Being a mom, it's just ... life changes. I swore it wouldn't but it did." She tipped her face into the air and screwed up her mouth tightly, as though she was making up her mind about something monumental.

"Tell you what," she said. "I'll come inside for a minute. We'll hang out."

A minute. That's what Ainsley was worth now.

"What about Justin?"

"Marguerite owes me. Her paperwork isn't exactly in order."

That was a little mean. But she was waiting for an answer.

"Mine is the second from last," said Ainsley.

CHAPTER THREE

As she turned the key and entered her rental apartment, Ainsley's stomach sank. All the horrific old feelings came rushing back.

Deirdre entered and placed her hands on her hips, surveying the room like a CSI agent.

"That couch needs to go."

She was right. It had been home base for eight solid weeks of Ainsley's depression. Near the end, she hadn't even been able to summon the energy to walk into her bedroom at night. She remembered waking up at four a.m. to a Lifetime movie flickering on the screen and an empty wine glass clasped to her chest.

"Maybe," said Ainsley. "New furniture is pretty low on my list of priorities."

"Overall, though, this place doesn't look as bad as I'd thought it would," said Deirdre. "You kept it pretty clean."

Ainsley pointed at her bag. "Can you take that into the bedroom? I have to get my mail."

Heading outside towards the mailboxes, Ainsley choked back a bitter taste in her throat. Entering her home had summoned the whole awful breakup again. Her husband hadn't even been decent enough to give her a face-to-face dumping. He'd just slunk off into the night, taking his clothes, books, and files.

Like a weasel.

A *legal* weasel.

Ainsley knew that if you take away someone's name, you take away his identity, his power. So she had sworn to never utter her husband's real name again. The Legal Weasel had become his new moniker.

Ainsley emptied her overflowing mailbox and carried the pile back into her unit and threw it on the table. Discount flyers, magazine offers, material from animal rights' advocacy groups. And several envelopes with three simple words printed on the front.

Your Statement Enclosed.

The balances printed inside those statements would constitute her final memories of the Legal Weasel.

Law school had seemed like ten years of education compressed into three. Those professors had knocked his brains around, and it'd been all he could do to not flunk out, much less hold a job. And Ainsley hadn't made enough money to support the both of them. So she'd been forced to charge groceries, clothing, gasoline, many of the necessities of life, to her various credit cards.

For three years, she'd lived this way.

Ainsley peeked into the second bedroom. There was the desk. She could still picture him, hunched over on a chair, his headphones jacked into his ears, his face buried in a textbook.

Nothing else was there now but an acoustic guitar. He'd barely been able to strum it. Right now, she couldn't remember anything he was good at. All she could think about were his failings.

But mostly she didn't want to think about him at all.

Deirdre's voice broke through her thoughts. "Ainsley, where is your laundry basket?"

She went into her bedroom. Deirdre had unzipped her bag and was separating the items into clean and dirty.

"You know I'm not blind," said Ainsley.

"Do you seriously not have a laundry basket?"

"I used to." Ainsley spun around. It must've been one of the things that the Legal Weasel had filched when he snuck out.

"All right," said Deirdre, "that's going on your birthday list." She typed a note into her phone.

"Thanks," Ainsley said, "but I can take it from here."

Deirdre stood back and watched her. "Did you ever regret getting married?"

Ainsley thought back.

She'd been ecstatic, over the moon, despite the fact that the wedding had been a cheapo event. They'd done the ceremony at a public park, the reception at a nearby steakhouse. Afterwards there had been a few envelopes slid into their hands, some helpful pieces of advice, don't worry about a honeymoon, now is the time to work, get yourself established, boy you should've seen how poor we were at the beginning, ha ha ha.

It'd all been music to her ears. She'd been totally in love, with him and the future.

How quickly things had changed.

"No," she said. "It was really good at first. Plus we never argued, not once."

"See, that's why it ended," said Deirdre. "I don't trust any couple that never argues. Me and Matt, we're like two cats in a bag."

Ainsley yawned. "Deirdre, I'm pretty tired, and I have to get ready to talk to my boss this afternoon."

"After seven days gone in the psych ward, I bet you do."

Deirdre picked up her heavy mom purse. "I've got to get home too. Why don't you text me tomorrow? We'll figure out a day to get lunch."

"Sounds good," Ainsley said.

"No, wait."

Deirdre was looking at her schedule on her phone. "I forgot to tell you—we're having a welcome back party for you on Saturday afternoon. At Waddington's Pub."

"Who is we?"

"Everybody."

Ainsley gazed into the future. The party would be nothing less than torturous. She'd have to explain herself, again and again, yes, I lost weight, no, he's not coming back, yes, just taking it one day at a time, no, my job still sucks, good to see you too, pat pat hug hug.

"You know," said Ainsley, "I'd rather not inconvenience anybody."

"Trust me, we're looking for a reason to get together anyways. You're the perfect excuse."

So that's what Ainsley had become. An excuse.

"Wear something pretty," said Deirdre. She kissed Ainsley on the cheek and left the unit. "Don't be a stranger."

The door closed behind her. Ainsley looked at her watch. It was only one o'clock. She needed to call work.

CHAPTER FOUR

Ainsley wanted to punch the green inflatable frog.

Slouched in a chair in the waiting area of her company's regional headquarters, she studied the weird amphibian in the corner. The vinyl thing was fixed on a weighted base, its belly grossly distended, a big red smile on its face. Its stubby amphibious arms were held up in a gesture of either surrender or aggression.

A sign across the frog's head read, *Tired of hopping from job to job? Apply for a position at Outfitz4ever. Hiring qualified team members now!*

Ainsley Walker chewed the inside of her cheek. This idiotic frog was speaking the truth to her.

She had been one of those job hoppers.

Over the last decade, she had worked as a receptionist, waitress, landscaper, secret shopper, warehouse shipping clerk, bookstore assistant manager, publisher's assistant, magazine researcher, and barista. And those were just the ones she wanted to remember. There were just as many that she wanted to forget about.

Recently, however, the truth was starting to sink in.

Twenty-nine years old, and nothing seemed to suit her. A small part of her had dreamed of falling in love, buying a small house, and baking pastries every afternoon.

None of that was happening, not soon, maybe not ever. Which is why, half a year ago, she had landed back in retail as a store manager. A mid-sized teenybopper clothing chain, Outfitz4ever boasted eighty-nine outlets nationwide. The stores specialized in selling six-dollar tops that disintegrated after three washings. Disposable fashion.

"Miss Walker," said a stern voice.

A matronly woman stood over her. She wore a St. John business suit and a poofy eighties hairstyle. She held her hands on her hips. This was Joanna, the regional manager.

"Nice to see you again," Ainsley said.

The regional manager tilted her head towards the hallway. "This way."

How curt. Ainsley had expected a bit more courtesy after spending a week in the loony bin.

She followed the boss down a gray hallway into an unremarkable office. Another woman, already seated on a folding chair in the corner, stood up and silently offered her hand. "This is Anna from HR," said Joanna. Ainsley shook her hand. The hairs on the back of her neck stood up.

The regional manager seated herself behind her desk and wasted no time. "We understand that there've been some problems at your location."

"Such as?"

"The payroll was six percent over this month."

Ainsley explained: "We went over because Kim called out sick seven days and I had to call in two extra shifts each day to cover her. Plus I was out all last week, as you know."

Joanna raised an eyebrow. "What was wrong with Kim?"

"Her four-year-old had a cold."

"So she called out sick for seven days?"

Ainsley shrugged. "That's what she said."

The boss wagged a stern finger. "Not good enough. *You* are the store manager. *You* need to get your employees into work."

Ainsley didn't know what to say. That she'd heard the part-timers gossiping about how Kim was out every night clubbing, courtesy of her sugar daddy? That getting dependable or even competent people into retail was next to impossible? That, after six months, this job was nothing like what she'd imagined—murder on her feet, deadening to her mind, demoralizing to her soul?

But all she could manage to say was, "Yes, ma'am."

"Now tell me about the drop in sales volume month-over-month."

"It's the construction," replied Ainsley. "The foot traffic in the mall is way down, everywhere. Parking is very limited. And nobody can talk over the jackhammers." She paused. "Frankly, the environment sucks. I wouldn't shop there either."

"So what have you done to overcome this problem?"

Ainsley shrugged. "I can't stop the construction."

"You could've talked to the mall manager."

"I did. There's nothing they can do either. Everybody's shopping online now anyways."

The regional manager gave her a significant glance, shook her head, then marked something in her notes. Ainsley wanted to spit in her face.

"Lastly," the woman said, "the bank deposit was sixty-three dollars short on Wednesday of last week."

"I was out all week."

"You're the store manager. You need to be on top of *everything*."

"I usually am." Ainsley scooted forward in her seat. "Joanna, maybe you're not aware, but I was an inch away from a major depression—"

"That is *irrelevant* to this discussion," the regional manager said sharply, glancing at Anna. "It is irrelevant. Am I making myself clear? I am only talking about your performance. It has been substandard."

It wasn't true. But Ainsley had a pretty good idea what was about to happen. She'd been through this before.

"We're terminating you," said the regional manager.

"Absolutely fantastic," said Ainsley. She chucked her pen backwards over her shoulder. It clattered on the carpet. Nobody moved to pick it up.

Anna handed Ainsley an envelope. "This," she said, "is your last paycheck, which includes your accumulated vacation hours."

Ainsley threw her head back and stretched out her arms towards the ceiling. "What an amazing year."

Joanna ignored it. "There's a separate severance check for five hundred dollars as well."

Ainsley couldn't think of anything to say. She'd been sandbagged. The deeper message of her firing, however, was that the regional manager didn't trust her anymore. She'd become a liability. There were lots of other perfectly non-depressed women salivating over a thirty-eight-thousand-dollar-a-year job with benefits.

Then something occurred to her.

Ainsley met the woman's eyes. "You don't think it's legally suspicious to fire me the day I get out of the psych ward?"

Joanna plastered her fakest smile. "I don't know what you're talking about."

"This five hundred dollars is your way of asking me to keep this out of court."

"Oh, get over yourself, Ainsley."

Joanna began straightening items, shuffling papers. Ainsley slapped the envelope against her knee impatiently.

She was trying to think of the perfect exit line, but her mind was a blank.

Instead, she left the office without a word. She stalked angrily down the hallway. This wasn't the end of the world. This had happened before. For years, employers had sensed her independence, her backbone, her absolute unwillingness to take any shit from people she considered beneath her. A few had fired her, others had just avoided her. She'd always kept her dignity.

But this one stung especially hard, mostly because of the timing.

On her way out of the lobby, she hauled back and socked the stupid frog straight in the mouth.

CHAPTER FIVE

Waddington's Pub was the type of sports bar that normally bored Ainsley. It'd been at least a year since she'd darkened its doorstep. Why had her friends chosen this place?

She scanned the bar. No less than fourteen television screens were suspended from the walls and ceiling, playing professional football games. Total snooze. The patrons were slightly more interesting. Every man over the age of twenty-five looked like a sloth with poor grooming habits. Ainsley felt a little disappointed. What was happening to her town?

More importantly, what was happening to her?

A waitress carrying a platter of deep-fried onion rings smiled at her. "You lookin' for somebody?"

"My friends are supposed to be having a party for me."

"Hm." She glanced across the room. "There's some people there. On the other side of the pool table."

Ainsley picked her way between the crowded tables, through the slurping, smacking, chewing, gulping. She tried to feel invisible.

The group numbered twenty. She counted nearly as many baby carriers as people.

She heard someone shout her name. Ainsley ducked her head in embarrassment. Chairs were scooted backwards. Women embraced her. Men squeezed her sideways under their armpits. *You all right?* Ainsley repeated all the rote explanations.

These had been her friends. Now they felt like strangers.

One, a former coworker from a job she could barely remember, said, "Ainsley, I am so sorry for everything. You must be devastated. Did you file yet?"

"No."

"Why not? He left *you*."

"I don't know. How hard is it to get divorced?"

"With no kids and no assets, it's piece of cake."

Soon the people trickled back to their seats, and Ainsley found the last open chair, at the distant end of the table, far from the overhead lights. Someone passed around a plate of wings. Ainsley couldn't summon an appetite yet. She sipped a white wine and listened to the conversation.

"I mean, it's like, *now* is the time, you know? She has *no* idea how *expensive* in-vitro gets—"

"Of course they didn't get into escrow, I told them don't bother looking, it's not going to happen with that FICO score—"

"All those years of hot tubbing, I had no idea what it was doing to his—"

"Did you know the worst thing about pregnancy is what happens to your feet, they're like loaves of bread—"

"Kevin loves his golf pro more than us, they text each other like high schoolers, he never even used to *like* sports—"

"I heard that they lost the deposit because the escrow wasn't licensed—"

"Maybe I'm, like, a crazy mother, but Noah's doo-doo actually smells *good*—"

Ainsley dipped a celery stick in a bowl of ranch dressing.

She studied it, turned it around. Wishing she could be anywhere but here, watching the slow creep of middle age, with its expanded waist sizes and shrunken dreams.

She was *not* ready to trade in her dreams.

A hand landed on her arm. It was Deirdre. "You're not talking today?"

Ainsley shrugged. "Lots of stuff going on."

"You're rebooting."

"We all are. I don't even recognize some of these people anymore."

The music started up from the PA system. A group of college-age kids were gathering on the dance floor nearby. "Do you want to dance?" asked Deirdre.

Ainsley shook her head.

"It'll make you feel better."

No, Ainsley thought, dancing didn't *cause* happiness, it was the *result* of happiness.

But Deirdre grabbed her hand. "Come on."

On the dance floor, Ainsley bounced a little and tried to smile. The bass pounded in her chest, the sleazy rapper's off-key chorus echoing in her ears. The girls surrounding them, their round faces still packed with baby fat, were twenty-two at most. They raised their arms and screamed at each other in the same pitch. It brought to mind drunken spring break group videos.

Ainsley lost her patience. She swallowed the last of her wine and went to the ladies' restroom.

She looked in the mirror.

Her arms were nearly toothpicks, her waist dangerously narrow. The face that looked back at her was neither young nor optimistic. The fine lines creasing the corners of her eyes angled downwards, not upwards. Her cheeks were starting to slide down.

Ainsley Walker wanted to stop her slide.

In every possible way.

She washed her hands thoroughly with soap. Then held them under the hand dryer until she gasped at the heat.

When she returned to the bar, her group was hugging, chatting, cleaning baby spit off shoulder towels. One guy was demonstrating his golf swing.

She stood nearby, coat in hand, waiting to be noticed, for someone to wish her goodbye.

Nobody did.

That sealed the deal. Ainsley walked towards the door. She cast one more glance back at the party. She caught Deirdre's eyes. She nodded. Deirdre sadly waved two fingers back.

CHAPTER SIX

Ainsley motored down the two-lane road. Back towards her cold, empty apartment. Mulling over her options in life.

She could pursue other jobs, but her resumé had become polluted with short-lived positions. There was always graduate school, maybe in criminology—but she'd have to pass the exams, which everybody said was impossible. And there was no guarantee that she'd even qualify for school loans.

Or there was exotic dancing. She nearly laughed out loud at the thought.

A familiar vehicle passing in the opposite direction caught her eye. It was a dark Nissan Altima, with an ugly dent under the front left panel.

She knew that dent. She had accidentally made it with a moving dolly.

It was *his* car. The Legal Weasel.

Ainsley pulled over to the shoulder. Watched its taillights shrink in her rearview. Her lips tightened, whitened. Deirdre had been right.

He was *still in town*.

She cranked the wheel, cut off an oncoming car, and

swung into the lane behind him. The Legal Weasel was five cars ahead of her. She craned her neck until she made out the license plate. He'd changed the number. That bastard had tried to cover his tracks.

Her fingers crushed the wheel in a death grip. Without a passing lane, she couldn't do anything but follow, and wait.

Suddenly the Nissan turned down a side street. She noted the name: Sycamore Avenue. Why Sycamore? Was this where his new woman lived? Ainsley wondered how attractive she was. She put on her blinker and turned after him.

She saw the Legal Weasel already pulling into a driveway half a block down. Ainsley screeched to a halt at the curb. In the driveway, the Nissan's taillights had just snapped off, which meant that the key was out of the ignition.

She leaped out and stalked up the driveway. Even through her fury, something didn't feel quite right. It might've been the children's playscape she glimpsed in the backyard. Or the baby seat in the back of the car.

A middle-aged woman stepped out, a bag of groceries in one arm. She was holding a toddler in the other.

Ainsley halted. The mother saw her and shrank back against her car.

"Don't hurt me," she said.

"You're not *him*," said Ainsley through her gritted teeth.

"Who?"

"My husband."

The mother shook her head. "Nothing but X chromosomes here."

Ainsley wiped the sweat from her face. She was starting to think more clearly now. "I saw your car, back there ... on the road. It ... looks just like my husband's car." She paused. "He left me three months ago."

"Well, that's when I bought it," the woman said. "A young guy sold it to me."

Ainsley felt her heart leap. "What was his name?"

"All I remember is that he just graduated from law school."

Christ, that was him. This *had been* his car. Ainsley sat down on the woman's lawn and placed her head in between her knees. For some reason this was hitting her hard. She felt like a new widow grieving.

"Did he say where he was going?"

The woman had closed her car door now, having accurately judged that Ainsley was no threat. "No. He just said he wouldn't need it anymore."

How useless. That could mean anything. He could've moved to New York, or shipped out to a foreign country. He could've splattered his brains against a wall. He could've even decided to just start taking the bus.

"I'm sorry to have scared you," Ainsley mumbled.

The woman shifted the toddler to her other arm. "Do you want to talk about this? I mean, I was a therapist before I had this little guy."

"No," said Ainsley. "Enjoy the car. It's a good one."

She stood up and shuffled back to the street. *Enjoy the car? It's a good one?* She couldn't believe how idiotic she sounded.

Inside her own vehicle, Ainsley thunked her head against the steering wheel. The woman's husband had come outside now. She could hear them talking, who was that, I'm fine, is she okay, I don't know.

No, Ainsley wanted to shout, *I am most definitely not okay*.

She needed to change her life.

CHAPTER SEVEN

If tracks were the same everywhere, Ainsley didn't know why running this one felt so difficult.

The four-hundred-meter loop was an oval strip of vulcanized rubber. Running alone in circles had felt ludicrous once she'd graduated from school, which is why she hadn't done it in years.

This morning, however, she wasn't alone.

She was following the rope-skinny frame of David Madradis, his legs switching through the air like a pair of chopsticks in sneakers. He'd been the Legal Weasel's classmate, had passed the bar immediately, and was now junior associate at a local law firm.

His specialty: divorce law.

"That's it," he shouted. He slowed to a walk and checked his watch. "Fourteen seconds over average. You slowed me down."

Ainsley couldn't even answer. She'd stopped running completely and was bent over at the waist, gasping.

"You'll get more air if you stand up," he said.

"My *God* was this easier in high school."

"No, it's always been hard."

In the same way that David had always been an argumentative prick, she thought. Ainsley and the Legal Weasel had gone out to dinner with him and his girlfriend once, a few years earlier. She'd been mortified when he'd haggled for nearly ten minutes over a fifty-nine-cent charge.

But she hadn't called him this week for a sympathetic shoulder. She'd called him for his legal advice.

Ainsley managed to catch up with him as they began the two-lap cooldown walk. David passed her a water bottle. She squeezed it over her head and tossed it back.

"So a six o'clock run was the only time you had available?"

"It's the life of a junior associate," he said. "My wife has started talking about me in the past tense."

"Believe me, I know the feeling," she said.

"Your husband was an interesting guy," said David. "Tall, smart, good-looking, occasionally charming."

"And a douchebag."

"It's often part of the package," he said.

"So you agree I need a divorce."

He nodded. "Your best bet is no-fault, no-signature."

"I'm fine with anything as long as it's easy and cheap."

He swung his lawyerly gaze towards her. "I incurred six figures of student loans based on the premise that divorce is *not* easy and *not* cheap."

"Then I'm going to need more water while you talk."

He passed the bottle back. "Where to begin? This state makes no-fault no-signature really difficult. We throw in lots of fun little hurdles." He began ticking off the list on his fingers. "First, they're going to need proof that you haven't seen or communicated with your husband in the last two months."

"But—"

"I know, it's impossible to prove an absence. Doesn't matter. You'll need to submit complete phone records. Next, they'll want to know that he hasn't been supporting you."

"He hasn't."

"Submit bank statements showing all account activity. Do you have any investments?"

"A mutual fund, but it's almost empty."

"You'll need to submit those records. Then the fun really begins."

"What's that?"

"The military. You'll need to write to all four branches of the military, plus the Coast Guard, for proof that your husband did not enlist."

"Why the hell—"

"Because our state has laws about women divorcing their husbands without their knowledge after they've enlisted. Our women can't be dumping good soldiers just because they ship out. It's bad for morale. But are you ready for the best one?"

"Okay."

"You have to prove you're not pregnant."

"What the—"

"Submit a receipt for purchase of birth control."

"But what if I'm not—"

"Then buy a package of condoms."

"Anything else?"

"Stop believing everything I say, Ainsley."

He looked over at her, one eyebrow arched. He was pulling her leg about that.

"Be serious, David."

"Okay. In all seriousness, the county fees can add up to over a thousand dollars. And notary public costs extra too." David thought for a moment. "You didn't sell your ring yet, did you?"

"No. It's at home."

"Good."

Ainsley smirked. "Let me guess why. I need to submit a time-stamped, date-stamped photo of me wearing it, and another of me not wearing it, to prove that I took it off."

"No, you might need to sell it to cover the cost of the filings. Lots of women do it that way."

"How long will all this take?"

"Eight months, minimum."

"I don't think that ring is worth as much as you think. Maybe we can work out a different payment plan. Would you prefer present thanks or future kindness?"

David shook his head. "I can't do anything official for you. I'm the new kid in the office, and all the paperwork has to go through the firm."

"Then I'll just hire you through the firm—"

He stopped her. "Don't. We charge an unbelievable rate. You can probably find someone new to do it for three grand."

Ainsley grew quiet. Three thousand dollars was the *cheap* way? She had a total of thirty-six dollars and nineteen cents in her bank account. Not to mention a month of back rent, another month due in two weeks, and all the assorted bills of a modern woman's life accumulated on her kitchen table.

"That's still too much."

David had dropped onto the bleacher seats. "Then you're in a pickle."

"A pickle only costs a few cents."

"Then you're in one of those really expensive deli pickles." He wiped his face on a towel. "It's been fun welcoming you to the swamp that is divorce law, but I've got to head out. Keep in touch, okay?"

He awkwardly clapped her on the shoulder, then left.

Ainsley watched David go. Then she stared out at the empty track, the same place that had hosted her early athletic victories. Those successes had faded long ago, were nothing but long-gone memories.

She was going to have to start somewhere.

CHAPTER EIGHT

Ainsley leaned back in her cheap home office chair and stretched her arms. The laptop screen waited without judgment.

She'd gone to the court website and downloaded most of the necessary forms. David had been right: a no-fault, no-signature divorce was difficult in this state. She was positive it wasn't this tough to get divorced in Nevada or California. Maybe that's why everybody out there split up so easily.

Ainsley yawned and spun around in the chair. She was wearing a bathrobe and her hair up in a messy bun. No makeup and constant dehydration and eight weeks of internal misery had amplified things to the point where she now hurried past mirrors with her head down.

And now she was overwhelmed, on top of it all.

She looked at the folder on her desktop. It had eleven different pdfs in it. All of them needed action from her, some more than others—and that was just amassing evidence.

Deep down, Ainsley didn't want to address any of them. That would mean addressing how her husband had walked out of her life, out of *his* life, out of *their* lives, without so much as a single word.

Ainsley played little invisible keyboard in the air with anxious fingers. The marriage hadn't been going great. She blamed him. It was a cliché, but in this case it really was the truth. He'd been uncommunicative, buried in law school textbooks, then buried in bar exam prep, then buried in his associate's position at the law firm. For the last year and a half, they'd felt like roommates. She'd carried the daily life of the relationship, while he'd carried its future.

That'd been the agreement—until he'd broken it.

The Legal Weasel.

Jared Christopher Walker.

She'd taken his last name as soon as they'd been married. It'd taken almost two years to change all the necessary documents. Now she was left with the utterly banal decision of whether to change it back.

Lurking behind that question was a more frightening one: What were the odds of finding a new husband? Should she save herself the work and just wait for number two? Did she even want a number two? And why, at the end, had the first one acted like such a number two?

She tabled those thoughts for now. They could be dealt with at another time.

What could she do here, now, tonight, in *this* moment, to push this divorce barge a little closer to its destination?

Her eyes scanned the list of documents.

The engagement ring.

She was going to have to sell it. It was the only way she could think of to get her hands on some easy money.

It wouldn't be hard. She could dig that out of storage, slide it to its former home past the second knuckle, and take it downtown to the jewelry district for a quick sale. Doing so might even make her feel better, oddly enough.

Ainsley went over to the bookshelf in her living room. Before she'd checked into the nuthouse, she'd stowed the engagement ring behind the female investigator mysteries on the second shelf, inside the plush box that it had come in from the jeweler. She loved hiding things there, behind the books. She used to stow concert tickets and cash there too, back before the world went paperless.

She removed the Sara Paretsky and the Sue Grafton titles. There: a little purple box. Ainsley felt her stomach sink to her shoes. She used to feel excited by the sight of that box, but now she felt a trepidation instead. It carried weight.

She picked up the box and studied it in her hand, but she didn't open it. Inside lay the ring, she knew. It was a simple gold band with stamped dimples, plus some pave. The diamond was special, however. Ainsley was a tough audience for diamonds, mostly because she knew too much about them, about their history, about the de Beers cartel, about price fixing.

But this diamond was two point one carats, more than twice the average size. It was also flawless. Normally, a person could see tiny veins, cracks, or inclusions inside most commercial diamonds.

Not this one. Hers was pure.

The seller was someone she'd known for years, a gemstone salesman who'd patiently answered all her questions on her many trips to the stalls and locked doors of the city's gemstone district downtown. One day, he'd called her about a special diamond that had crossed his desk. Ainsley had begged him to hold it for her. The next weekend, she and the Legal Weasel had made a special trip to look at it. He'd bought it then and there, with little regard to cost. She'd worn it with pride for the next four years.

Ainsley opened the purple box. She'd take it for one last spin before losing it forever.

To her surprise, the box was empty.

———

Ainsley stood there, dumbfounded. This had to be a mistake.

She'd put the ring in the box before she'd left. That was certain. The moment was clear in her mind. She'd been in the kitchen, eating peanut butter from the jar, talking on the phone with Deirdre. Ainsley had been telling her about the ring, how she couldn't stand to look at it, how she needed help. Deirdre had told her to put it back in the box and hide it away.

So Ainsley had done that. She'd placed the ring inside the box and carried it over to the bookshelf and put it behind her books.

She hadn't imagined that.

Now Ainsley stepped back, looked at the shelf. She had well over a hundred paper books, mostly mystery and thriller novels, plus even more on her e-reader. She'd always connected with those types of stories. Romance was lovely if you could find it, but it was secondary, in her mind, to a person's mission.

Maybe the ring had fallen out. Shelf by shelf, Ainsley pulled out all of her books and placed them onto the floor. Then she looked.

Nothing.

Maybe it fell down behind the bookcase. She went to the wall and placed the side of her face against it. She squinched one eye shut, turned on the flashlight on her phone, and shone it in the gap between the bookcase and the wall.

Nothing.

Cursing under her breath, she began to walk in slow circles around her coffee table.

None of this made sense.

Rings didn't just get up and disappear. She'd placed it there a little less than two weeks ago, just before the voluntary psychiatric hold.

Maybe she really had lost her mind. Could she have hallucinated the entire episode?

Ainsley dialed Deirdre. Her friend picked up on the third ring in mid-sentence with her toddler.

"—no, you have to put the rest of toy back, Justin, not just part of it, all of it, right there in the box like that—hey Ainsley what's up?"

"Did we have a conversation about my engagement ring a couple weeks ago?"

"I can't even remember what happened on the television episode I watched last night," her friend replied.

"Think back, please—it's important."

Deirdre sighed. She grew quiet. "I remember you telling me that you couldn't stand to even look at your engagement ring."

"Yes," said Ainsley, "exactly. And what did you advise?"

"I told you to put it back in the little plush jeweler's box that it came in."

"And where did I say I was going to put it?"

"I don't remember. Wait, did you *lose* the ring?"

Ainsley sat down on the sofa. "Not exactly. I just don't know where it is."

"That's not losing it?"

"I didn't misplace it. I have the box, but the box is empty."

"Holy shitballs," said her friend. "Are you sure you put it in the box?"

"Yes!"

"Okay! Well, it can't have walked out by itself. Are you thinking that someone may have stolen it?"

"I mean—it's impossible, right?" said Ainsley. "Nobody

has the key to this apartment except the landlord. She's an old woman who doesn't even live in-state."

"But somebody else does."

There was a pregnant pause. Then Ainsley said, "You mean *him*?"

"It makes sense, doesn't it?"

Ainsley grew frustrated. "No, it doesn't. How would he even know that I was on a psychiatric hold?"

"Maybe they called him. It's probably routine to inform the spouse."

Ainsley felt herself break out into a cold sweat. "Even so, why would he sneak into his separated wife's home and steal back her engagement ring?"

"Maybe because he knew you were gone. He knew he wouldn't get caught."

"But why?"

"I don't know. Probably to sell it?"

Ainsley closed her eyes and ground her palm into her forehead. "That is not like him at all. He didn't care that much about money. He didn't even touch our joint bank account, and that has three thousand dollars in it."

The sound of a crash. "Now look what happened, Justin, baby, you have to be *careful* honey—hey Ainsley, okay, it doesn't have to make sense. Maybe he's just lost his mind?"

"Maybe."

"He walked out on you with no explanation, no forwarding address. That's crazy anyways, right?"

"Yeah."

The toddler began to scream. "I'm gonna have to call you back."

"Okay, no worries."

Ainsley ended the call. She looked around her humble two-bedroom apartment.

Before she leapt to conclusions, she would search her entire home, top to bottom.

CHAPTER NINE

In the elevator, Ainsley could feel the man's eyes upon her.

The two of them were alone in the elevator going up to her disappeared husband's former law firm. He wore a blue business suit and had a face that begged for your money and your trust.

Ainsley clasped her leather folder close to her chest, waiting for the floor to arrive.

Then he spoke. "Aren't you Jared's wife?"

"I was," she said.

"I'm Kevin, one of his colleagues. Former colleagues. I think we met at the holiday party."

"Maybe."

"If you don't mind me asking, we've all been wondering what happened there. I mean, he just straight up disappeared?"

Ainsley looked straight ahead. "I was hoping to ask all of you the same question."

"Where did he go?"

"I don't know," she said, spitting out every syllable.

The doors opened. Ainsley stepped out into the fourth-floor lobby of the Miller & Co law firm. It wasn't a large company—only about twenty lawyers total—and it wasn't particularly expensive or prestigious either. They did local work, mostly commercial disputes as well as some securities fraud litigation.

It was, however, the place that the Legal Weasel had most recently worked. Until he'd quit his job the same day that he'd disappeared.

Ainsley walked to the reception area. The woman behind the desk was wearing a headset and didn't look up as she approached. "May I help you," she stated flatly.

"I have an appointment with Irene Grackley."

"One moment, may I ask your name?"

"Ainsley Walker."

"Oh," she said, looking up. "I'll let her know you're here."

Ainsley took a small paper cup of coffee and stood in the waiting area. Attorneys raced up and down the hallways, dressed in more pinstriped business suits. Her disappeared husband had owned three of them. He rotated them throughout the week. Ainsley had picked them up from the drycleaners for him.

A sixtyish woman came striding into the waiting area. She had well-combed gray hair and a brisk attitude, friendly but professional. Ainsley had met her before too, at holiday functions and spouse days, but they'd never had anything more than brief conversations.

"Ainsley," she said, hand outstretched, "it's good to see you again, even under such circumstances. You said you had some questions about Jared."

"I do," she said.

"Let's see if I can answer them."

Ainsley followed the human resources officer back to her office and sat down on the sofa. Irene sat at her desk and turned sideways in the seat to face Ainsley. She crossed one leg over the other, folded her hands, and looked at her visitor.

"So," she began.

"So," answered Ainsley.

"What would you like to know?"

"He quit his job on the eighth of March," Ainsley said.

The human resources officer consulted a document. "Yes, he notified me on March eighth that he was leaving our employment, immediately."

That was the same day he'd disappeared from the home, taking some of his things as well. It'd been a terrible day.

"No forewarning," Ainsley said.

"None. It's not necessary."

"Did he explain himself at all? In any way?"

The woman shook her head no. "I didn't even see him. He left the document on my desk while I was at lunch. He also emailed it to me at that time."

"Did he give a change of address?

"No."

"Did he give a forwarding address?"

"I don't believe so," she said. "Are you going to treat this as a missing person case?"

"No, I'd prefer not to," replied Ainsley. "He clearly made a plan, and he executed it."

"It's very odd," she said.

"Was he happy here?"

Irene hedged. "I can't reveal the contents of our employee evaluations."

"I don't mean what you thought of him. I mean did he ever tell *you* that he was unhappy here?"

"No, not that I can remember. What did he say to you?"

"He didn't tell me anything," said Ainsley. "That was kind of the problem."

"I see. What else do you need?"

Ainsley sighed. "An address."

"You've tried calling him, obviously."

She nodded. "He changed the number."

"I am bound by the laws of confidentiality," she said, "but if I were you, I'd probably start to look out of state."

"There is something you're not telling me."

"I can't reveal that."

Ainsley edged to the front of her seat. "Woman to woman, I'm really hurting here. I need some answers. I also need to get my ring, which I think he stole."

A compassionate look crossed Irene's face. "I'm sorry, but that's all I know. We're in the dark too." She paused. "He was respected here."

"But he wasn't liked."

Irene made a small head tilt. It was neither a confirmation nor a denial. But Ainsley knew what that meant.

"Thanks for your time," she said.

They shook hands. Ainsley exited the office and made her way back towards the lobby.

"Ainsley," a voice said. She turned and saw Kevin, the colleague from the elevator, striding towards her down the hallway. He was carrying a cardboard box.

"Yes?"

"We found this in Jared's office after he left. He evidently was in a rush and forgot a few things."

He handed her the small box. "Thank you," she said.

The attorney nodded warmly. "Just trying to help you out. If you need a private investigator, I can recommend a good one."

As Ainsley descended the elevator, she clutched the box to her side. She didn't need to hire an investigator.

She was going to *become* an investigator.

CHAPTER TEN

Ainsley sat at her kitchen table and stared at the cardboard box. The object lay there, neatly taped, a silent container that promised answers to her all-consuming personal mystery.

And yet she couldn't bring herself to open it.

Why had he left it in his office? The only answer was that he'd been in such a rush the day that he left—he quit his job at lunchtime and was out of everybody's life by three o'clock pm—that he'd just plain forgotten the thing. Ainsley knew that the Legal Weasel had a fairly poor memory. He could analyze but couldn't remember much. His desk was always a mess of Post-It notes and cryptic words and numbers scrawled on scraps of paper.

Taking a deep breath, she used a pair of scissors to cut open the box. She reached inside and felt around.

She removed a small white ceramic cat. She'd bought it for him years ago. There was a drunken backstory—they'd giggled over it for no reason at all in a craft store—but she hadn't realized that he'd kept it, all this time. Ainsley wiped away a tear with the heel of her palm.

Then she removed a Rubik's Cube. It wasn't finished. He

never could finish it. The Legal Weasel didn't think three-dimensionally. He could barely throw a ball either.

Other objects emerged in a curious procession. A magnetic paperclip holder. A tattered copy of *Wine Spectator* magazine. A random menu from an Indian restaurant.

She fished out a bag of saltwater taffy. The label read *Boardwalk Taffy Company (est. 1877)*. She hadn't known that he liked taffy or kept a stash of it. After that came a Miami Dolphins mug. He didn't care about football—or so she thought.

She sat back. Nothing in here gave any clues to his whereabouts, but they did give a clue to something else.

Ainsley realized there was a lot she didn't know about her disappeared husband.

––––––

Ainsley sat at her kitchen table staring at her phone. She'd opened the contacts list, scrolled down to the name.

Robin Thompson.

Her sister-in-law. The Legal Weasel's older sister.

She lived in Mahwah, New Jersey, outside of New York City, with her husband Wayne, and their three kids. They were a busy family, and distance plus lack of time had prevented Ainsley from building a relationship with them. It didn't help that their only shared link, her disappeared husband, had also failed to keep in close touch with his sister's family.

But she and Robin had always been friendly. They'd already spoken once, about a week after he'd disappeared. Robin had been just as flummoxed as Ainsley. Maybe it was Ainsley's imagination, but she felt that this was pulling them closer together.

Life was weird like that.

Ainsley inhaled deeply. Then she hit the telephone icon and switched the call to speakerphone.

To her surprise, Robin answered on the first ring. "Ainsley!"

"Hi Robin," she said. "I hope I'm not disturbing you."

"I'm just trying to clean up around here. It's a never-ending task."

"How are Wayne and the kids?"

"They're all good. Maiah just performed in *Honk* at school. She played the moorhen best friend."

"I don't know what you just said, but I'm sure you're proud."

"Oh yeah—she did great. Now she's been bitten by the acting bug."

"It gets a lot of people."

An awkward pause. "So I know why you're calling. I'm afraid I can't be very much help."

Ainsley's teeth were set on edge. "You haven't seen or heard from him?"

"He messaged me to let me know that he's fine and that he's traveling."

"That all he said?"

"That's it."

"Robin, your brother stole my engagement ring. The one he bought for me."

There was no sound from the other end of the line. "Well —how do you know that?"

"It was taken from my apartment while I was gone for a week."

"It could've been somebody else—"

"Nothing else was taken, Robin. And only two people have the key. Your brother, and the elderly landlord who lives out of state."

A note of desperation crept into Robin's voice. "What do you want me to do? Apologize on his behalf? He's an adult."

"I just need you to help me find him."

"I don't know where he is, Ainsley."

She struggled to remain calm. "Are you telling me the truth, Robin?"

The woman sighed. "I don't appreciate you making me choose between you and my brother."

That much was true. Ainsley was forcing her hand. But she wanted to recover her engagement ring. And she wanted to know what had happened to her husband. It was a tickle in the back of her head that she couldn't quite scratch.

"I agree that he's put us in an awkward position," Ainsley said. "I didn't choose this and neither did you."

"That much is true."

"Will you promise to tell me if you hear anything from him?"

"Sure."

"Thanks."

They chatted for a minute longer, then ended the call. Ainsley had the uneasy sense that Robin had chosen to side with her brother.

CHAPTER ELEVEN

Snap crackle pop.

It sounded like music. Popping, hissing, spitting—these were the final melodies of a chopped-up acoustic guitar as it went up in flames.

Ainsley shut her eyes and tried to enjoy the sounds. But burning this instrument hadn't made her feel as happy as she'd thought it might.

She was sitting alone in an Adirondack chair at the outdoor firepit in the common area of her apartment complex. Orange firelight played with shadows across her face.

Clutched in her hands was a bottle of gin. Normally she was a fan of the crushed grape, but tonight the only alcohol in her apartment had been a half bottle of the best of the juniper bush. She'd warmed a can of frozen orange juice from concentrate in a saucepan, then carefully drizzled it through the narrow opening into the gin bottle.

This was low-class, no doubt—and she didn't care.

She was halfway through the concoction. And unless Jimmy Buffett had been brought back to life and was performing nearby, Ainsley guessed that she was soon going to become the drunkest person in a twenty-mile radius.

She leaned her head back against the chair. She'd had run into a dead end in her life. She hadn't made headway in finding her husband. She was unemployed. People were sympathetic, but nobody was willing to give much more than lip service to her problems. Her bank account was getting dangerously low.

Ainsley had fallen through the cracks. She'd become one of those silent failures.

The only thing that made her feel better was the knowledge that there were a lot of other people who'd fallen through the cracks too. At least, that's what she kept telling herself.

Then her phone rang.

Startled, she fished it out of her pocket and looked at the screen. *Unknown caller.* Area code 201.

That was probably a robocall. She shouldn't pick up, but she decided to do so anyways.

"Yello," she said.

"Ainsley, this is Wayne Thompson. Robin's husband."

Her brother-in-law. She sat up in the chair. She didn't know that Wayne even had her number. They'd never spoken outside of family group events. He was a senior systems admin at a trading firm, which meant that his time was limited. During his rare free moments apart from job, kids, and wife, he usually retreated to his ham radio setup in the basement.

"Wayne?" she said.

"I bet you're surprised to hear from me."

"Well, yeah—"

He sounded like he was breathing hard.

"Are you going somewhere?" she said.

"I'm walking the dogs right now. It's the only time I can find privacy these days."

"What's going on?"

"First, I want to tell you how sorry I am for what Jared's put you through. You didn't deserve any of this."

Ainsley felt herself start to melt inside. Tears formed in the corners of her eyes. Finally someone had recognized the size of the shit sandwich that she'd been unjustly served.

"Thank you," she choked out.

"I know we don't talk, you've got your life and we've got ours."

He trailed off into silence. She could hear him breathing heavily. "Yes? What is it?"

"Ainsley, I don't know exactly how to say this—but my wife lied to you."

Her entire body froze. "So she told you that I called her."

"Yeah, and she told you that she hadn't seen Jared. That's not true. We've seen Jared. Two weeks ago."

"How?"

"He stayed with us for three days."

Now Ainsley was on her feet, the gin a distant memory. She began pacing the grass near the fire. "That's interesting. Tell me more."

"First, did he really steal your engagement ring?"

"I have to believe so," she replied.

"Tell me."

She explained the situation.

"I could get in a lot of trouble for talking to you," he said, "but Jared has never been straightforward with me. I work with congenital liars and can spot them in a second. I'm glad that he's out of your hair."

"Me too."

"You're not trying to get him back?"

She sighed. "I just want to know what is happening with him. I also really want my engagement ring."

"But you don't want him back?"

"That's a tough question."

"He wouldn't tell me much. He said you two weren't getting along and he didn't like his job and he needed to rethink everything."

"That's it?"

Wayne's breathing was coming in spurts now. "Sorry, this dog is energetic. Okay, the last night Jared was there, he and Robin were talking in private in the study. They had the door closed. She wouldn't tell me anything and it was honestly pissing me off."

Every hair on Ainsley's arms was standing up on end. "And?"

"He came out to get a drink in the kitchen and when he left ... that's when I noticed his phone on the kitchen counter. He'd left it."

"What did you do?"

"I did what a good systems admin does. I picked it up and noticed that the screen lock timeout hadn't begun yet. He had it set on sixty seconds."

"So you closed it?"

His voice grew serious. "No, I went to his Google Maps and enabled location sharing with my email address."

Ainsley nearly dropped her own phone. Her hand clutched itself into a fist. This was exactly the break that she needed.

"Are you telling me that you have full access to his location?"

"That's right."

"For how long?"

"Either until he notices what I've done, or until he gets rid of the phone."

"He won't notice," said Ainsley. Her husband was oblivious when it came to his personal items. His mind had always been elsewhere.

"So for quite a while. Have you told Robin?"

Wayne laughed. "Of course not. She wouldn't approve."

"Is it legal?"

"Technically, no. But I do this all the time at work with our employees. I did the same to Robin's phone and the kids' phones too, no permissions asked. And for Jared, I used a burner email, so he can't trace it back to me. At least, not easily."

Ainsley danced a little jig around the fire, then stumbled, nearly falling into the flames. She straightened herself out.

"You've made my night, Wayne."

"You're welcome. Your night is about to get even more interesting."

"Because—"

"—I can tell you—"

"—where he is right now," she finished. "Where?"

"Hotel Poseidon, Miami Beach. He arrived there two days ago."

So the woman at the law firm had been right. Ainsley struggled to think of a single reason why her ex-husband would've headed to Miami. He'd never visited south Florida before. In fact, the Legal Weasel hadn't much liked leaving home at all, which caused some stress in their relationship. Ainsley had grown up with a traveler for a father, and her fondest memories had been accompanying him on journeys.

"You are a prince," she said.

"I'm actually a scoundrel."

"Then why are you doing this?"

"Because I don't trust Jared. Robin's not telling me a thing and I don't like not knowing. It's to protect myself too."

"You know I have to go to Miami now."

"Whatever you do, do *not* mention me," he replied. "We never spoke. Make something up."

"Of course," she said. "If he moves, you'll tell me?"

"You bet. I'm almost home, Ainsley. I gotta run."

"I owe you so much, Wayne."

"Be good."

He disconnected. Ainsley immediately dumped the remaining gin-and-juice onto the fire, dousing it. Then she ran back to her apartment and pulled up a travel website on her phone.

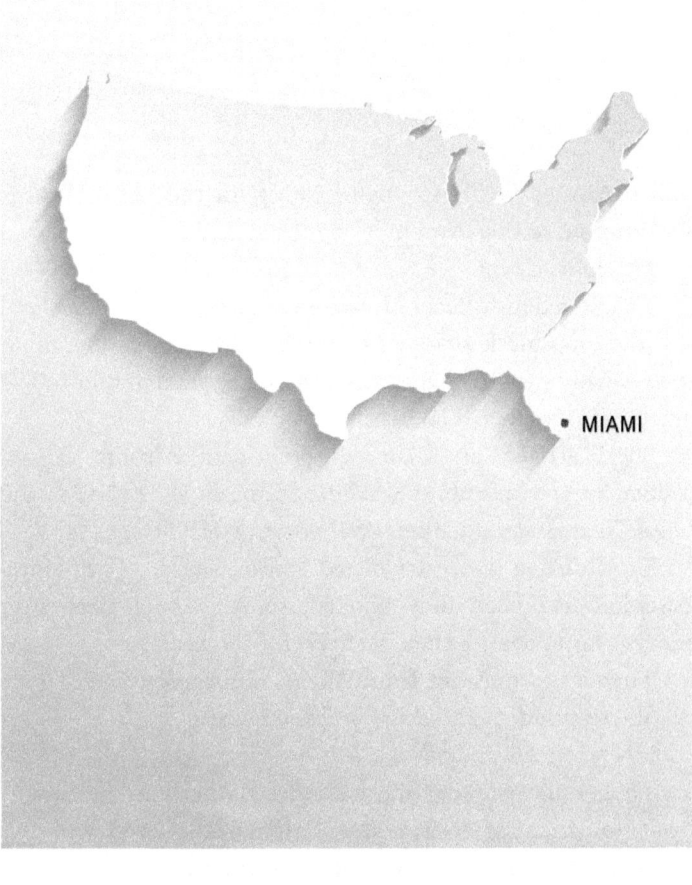
MIAMI

CHAPTER TWELVE

When Ainsley finally stopped looking for the Legal Weasel, she'd run more than four miles on the strand.

No sight of him.

This was South Beach. It was four-thirty in the afternoon, and the long black shadows of the beachfront condominium towers had begun to fall across the orange sand and onto the blue ocean waters to the east.

She'd arrived at Miami International Airport at ten o'clock in the morning. Wayne had messaged her that the Legal Weasel was at Collins Avenue and 178th Street.

She took a taxi down to South Beach. The Hotel Poseidon had been fully booked, so Ainsley checked into another hotel nearby, then beelined for the beach.

Then a text message from Wayne. *He's moving south.*

She responded: *I need more frequent updates!*

His reply: *I have a job, Ainsley.*

Then radio silence. She'd wandered the winding beachfront for the last four hours. Scanned the sand and the crowds. She'd gone down to the tip of the island, to South of Fifth, aka SoFi. There it'd been mostly wealthy Europeans.

You could identify them by their thin-soled footwear and light sweaters tied around their necks. Then she'd gone up north, where she'd passed through the Argentines, speaking their peculiar Spanish.

One thing was in common: beautiful people were everywhere. The models wearing pink Lycra, gliding on inline skates like swift but silent deities. The male peacocks strutting around the weightlifting area, their tanned muscles oiled and glistening.

South Beach was alluring, but it wasn't doing any favors for her self-esteem.

Ainsley herself was wearing a simple exercise bra with a loose white tank top, baggy blue jogging shorts, and basic sneakers. She'd packed so quickly that she hadn't given much thought to appearances. She honestly didn't care about what people thought about her, not at this period in her life.

That was fine. Ainsley felt like a cast-iron pan. Nobody could burn her because she'd already been scorched. Being dumped by your husband, for no reason, had that effect.

"Ainsley?" said a voice.

She turned in a heartbeat. A thirtyish man with a salt-and-pepper beard was sitting astride a fat-tired beach cruiser. He wore a wide-brimmed sun hat, tropical board shorts, and flip-flops.

"Do I know you?" she said.

"You don't remember me, do you?" he said. "We used to work together."

She squinted at the man, trying to place him. Ainsley had held so many different jobs, encountered so many different colleagues. She drew a blank.

"The bookstore," he said.

That was it. She'd been an assistant manager at an independent bookstore, and he'd been a part-timer for a few months during that time. She remembered him as younger, skinnier, and more clothed.

"You worked on weekends," she said. "You had another job during the week."

"I was a doctoral student."

"That's right. Did you ever finish?"

He shook his head sadly. "I lost interest."

Ainsley snapped her fingers. "I remember now! We used to make fun of the terrible covers on the bestseller list. Right?"

Paul's face lit up. "Exactly. You liked mystery and adventure—"

"And I caught you reading really bad Regency romance—"

He covered his face in mock despair. "Oh God, why do you remember that?"

"You know, the one thing I don't remember is your name."

"Paul. Paul Ochoa."

They shook hands. His was large and a bit soft.

"Nice to meet you again, Paul. What are you doing in Miami?"

"I moved here about five years ago. You still back home?"

"Yeah."

"On vacation?"

"No. I'm looking for someone."

Paul leaned his forearms across his handlebars and studied her. "Well, you look good doing it."

Ainsley wasn't having any of that. "Thanks. It's been nice talking to—"

He cut her off. "Maybe I can help you."

"I don't think so."

"I work in property management. I have a lot of contacts in the city."

Ainsley looked at him. Back then, Paul had been a nerdy academic type. Today, he appeared to have changed, and his intentions weren't entirely clear. It was safer to go on her way alone. But hadn't she come here to find her engagement ring?

"I suppose," she said.

"Let's talk about it tonight over dinner," he said.

"No time," she replied, "this is urgent." Ainsley decided to lay her cards on the table. "It's my husband. We're separated, and he stole my engagement ring. I want to get it back."

Paul quirked an eyebrow up. "You want to get the ring back, or the husband?"

"The ring."

"What about the husband?"

That was the gold-plated question, really. Ainsley knew she wanted a divorce, but she also knew that could change, depending on what he brought to their next conversation. Either way, their relationship would never be the same. The relationship had been wounded.

"That's between me and him," she said.

Paul swung a leg off his bicycle and motioned for her to walk. Without any better options, she followed him.

————

"Miami is a place people come to disappear," he said. "But my property management firm manages seven different buildings here. Where was he today?"

"All I know is that he spent the morning at Collins and 178th Street."

"That's Sunny Isles Beach," said Paul. "What was he doing there?"

"I have no idea."

"That's where all the ghost condos are."

"What are those?"

Paul high-fived a young woman gliding by in a bikini on a

skateboard. "Russians buy condos for investment and never live in them."

"Oh."

"Was your husband affiliated with the mob?"

"No, of course not."

"What's his job?"

"Attorney. Commercial transactions and fraud."

He looked over the tops of his sunglasses at her.

"What?" said Ainsley.

"Are you sure he wasn't affiliated with the mob?"

"I don't know," she said, exasperated. "He disappeared suddenly. He left me, and he left his job on the same day."

Paul made an *mmm* sound. Then chose his words carefully. "Something changed him."

"Yeah."

"Here's what I can do," he said. "I can put the word out in my groups and see if anybody up there gave him a tour of a condo."

"He wouldn't have bought a condo," said Ainsley.

"He wouldn't have left you and his job in the same day either," said Paul. "Now, in return, you'll come out with me tonight. We can talk books."

She sighed. This was a light blackmail: exchanging access for time.

"I can't," she said. "I'm going to be at his hotel, looking for him."

"Which one?"

"The Poseidon."

"They have a bar in the lobby. I'll meet you there at seven pm."

Ainsley quit resisting. She hadn't chosen this situation, but it'd chosen her.

"Fine," she said.

"Now give me your number," he said, his phone already out.

Ainsley told him, and he entered it. This was starting to feel like a quasi-date. She was still quasi-married, so at least the two things corresponded.

"What's your husband's name?"

She told him that too.

"I'll see you tonight," said Paul. He leaned over and stole a kiss on her cheek before she could react. Then he took off on his fat-tired beach cruiser.

Ainsley watched him go. Miami changed people. In her mind, he was still the quiet graduate student slicing open boxes of hardbacks and pushing the stock cart through the store.

She wondered if that was still true.

CHAPTER THIRTEEN

In the lobby of the Poseidon, Ainsley held her lemonade cocktail in one hand and looked at her phone on the table.

No word from Wayne all afternoon. The Legal Weasel could've left the city for all she knew. But if he was still here, he'd have to pass through this lobby at some point. And she would see him.

She'd thought about talking to the Poseidon hotel staff, then dismissed the idea. They were legally obligated to protect their guests' privacy. If they suspected Ainsley of stalking her estranged husband—even if she was in the right —she wouldn't be allowed to sit here in the lobby. It was easier to play the barfly with one eye peeled on the elevators.

Seven o'clock had come and gone. No sign of Paul. She hadn't expected anything to come of it. People in Miami were notorious flakes, men and women alike. What they felt one minute would change like the breeze and you'd be forgotten.

But Ainsley was built different. Her feelings were strong, sometimes too strong, and they didn't dissipate. She didn't switch horses midstream. She committed to things—and stayed committed.

Across the lobby, a small gift shop was open. A bored girl was on her phone behind the cash register. On display was a set of mugs. One was of the Miami Dolphins.

She thought back to the box of items from the Legal Weasel's office. There'd been a Miami Dolphins mug.

Ainsley tilted her head and narrowed her eyes. She had so many questions.

A guy sidled up to her at the bar. "Sweetheart," he said, "are you looking for something tonight."

"I am," she said, "but you don't have it."

"The lesbian bar is further up the street," he sneered, then moved away.

Ainsley rolled her eyes and went back to elevator watch. The doors were shutting on a man. She could only see him from behind, but at first glance he looked like the Legal Weasel—normal height, thin build, brown hair. Truth be told, he looked a lot like many other people.

"I'll be right back," she said to the bartender.

She moved swiftly across the lobby to the elevator. Ainsley had changed into a spaghetti-strap top, a denim miniskirt, and cute white sneakers. She'd dressed more for comfort in the heat than anything.

The elevator was ascending. She stood watching the red lights on the panel. It stopped at the sixth floor and stayed there for a good while. Then it came back down again. The doors slid open. It was empty.

If that was him, he was staying on the sixth floor.

A couple stepped past her into the elevator. She followed them.

"What floor?" the man said.

"Sixth," she replied. "Thanks."

The elevator stopped at four. The couple left, and the elevator proceeded on its way to the sixth. Ainsley stepped out. She found herself at the end of a long corridor, doors lining both sides. At the other end was a silhouette of a man at an ice machine. The distant sound of crunching reached her ears as the ice filled his bucket.

From here, it looked very much like her husband.

Ainsley opened her mouth to shout, but her throat felt like sandpaper and his name wouldn't come out. Instead, she walked towards him, professionally, like an investigator.

Not like a wife.

The man finished the ice collection, and his figure disappeared down a perpendicular hallway. Ainsley's eyes widened. She couldn't lose him. Running now, she took the corner sharply—just in time to hear a door close.

Her heart dropped. She was looking at another long corridor, at least twenty rooms, ten on each side. He could be in any of them.

Ainsley's arms dangled loosely by her side. This was just her luck. It wouldn't do to knock on every door. But maybe she could draw him out with one of their favorite songs.

They both loved a Disney children's song from the nineties, one from the movie about the mermaid who trades her voice for legs. They used to sing it to one another, then giggle.

Back in happier times.

She strolled down the hallway, her voice singing loud. Ainsley couldn't carry a tune in a bucket, but no matter. The melody should be enough to pull him out of his room, if he was there.

Ainsley made it to the end of the hallway. No reaction from the silent hotel rooms. So she returned down the corridor, singing again. *It's possible she wants you too*.

She'd watched that movie countless times after her dad had passed.

One of the room doors opened. A black woman stuck her

head out into the hallway. "Who is that butchering one of my favorite songs?"

"Does it sound that bad?" said Ainsley.

"You better take some lessons before you walk around like that."

"I appreciate that."

The door shut. Ainsley went back to the elevator and pressed the down button. She thought of her soon-to-be ex-husband.

If her estranged husband was on this floor, he didn't wanna kiss the girl. And he didn't miss the girl either. Not one bit.

———

Back at the lobby bar, Paul was waiting for her. "You probably didn't think I was coming."

"You're right about that."

"Hey, I wasn't sure if I was coming. This afternoon has been crazy." He checked his phone anxiously.

Ainsley figured out the situation. "What's her name?"

"Who?"

"The girl who's not answering you about going out tonight."

It was just a guess, but she hit a bullseye. Paul sighed. "Luana."

Ainsley kept a straight face. "I bet she's a model."

He cast his face down and nodded.

"Brazilian girls are different." Paul looked up. "That's okay. Girls like her are everywhere around here."

Ainsley wasn't offended. She was acquainted with all the usual tricks—applying the smoky eye, the cinching, the squeezing, the shaving. Even so, she knew she wouldn't be winning Miss Universe anytime soon, especially not in Miami. Here, she was barely a footnote.

Ainsley liked it that way. Her mind wasn't on dating right now, to put it lightly.

"Did you find anything about Sunny Isles?" she said.

"Your ex-husband took a tour of the Crystal Sparkle tower," Paul said. "And he was with a woman."

Ainsley felt her blood begin to boil. "What type of woman?" she spit out slowly, each syllable coated in anger.

"They can't give the woman's name out. All I know is that they left as soon as the tour ended and didn't follow up on any messages about buying."

Ainsley's imagination carried her away to some terrible places. She imagined a gorgeous model on his arm, a side chick that he'd kept secret from her—

"Miss, you're going to strangle that thing," said the bartender. His eyes glanced at her hand. It had her glass in a death grip.

She relaxed. "Sorry."

Then her phone's notification beeped. Ainsley quickly read the screen.

Wayne had texted. *Now he's at 23rd St, west of 2nd Ave. Wynwood. Address checks out as a nightclub called Cancha Luna.*

Then:

Going to bed now. ;-)

Ainsley quickly replied and thanked him. Then she looked up.

"I may not be as pretty as your model, but do you want to take this ordinary chick out clubbing tonight?"

Paul's eyes flicked down to her phone. "You know where he is?"

"My source tells me he's on Twenty-Third street, west of Second Avenue."

"That's Wynwood. That's a scene."

"It's a club called Cancha Luna."

Paul nodded. "I've heard of it."

She looked at the man with a small smirk on her lips. "Be my wingman, Paul. I need your protection."

"What do I get?"

"A sense of satisfaction. And I'll make sure to look hot so the other women want to steal you from me."

He grinned. "That's a deal."

"Stay here. I'll go back to my hotel and change. It's only two blocks away."

"How long?"

"Twenty-five minutes, tops."

"I'll still be here."

"Don't make any promises you can't keep. The Brazilian could still call."

He smirked. "I don't remember you being this tough, Ainsley."

"We all change, Paul."

"We do."

Ainsley dropped a bill for the bartender on the counter and left the lobby.

CHAPTER FOURTEEN

Ainsley strode into the Cancha Luna nightclub with a single-minded purpose. She'd changed into a simple blue one-piece dress but kept the white sneakers. She hadn't brought any heels. Plus, she wanted to be ready for anything, including a chase.

The nightclub was essentially a large warehouse, part indoors, part outdoors. On its surface, it seemed like a decent place. There was a DJ booth at one end. Colorful lasers criss-crossed the ceiling. Raised platforms for dancing. Something else, however, was different from home.

The clientele.

Most of the people looked like sewer rats. Stringy hair coated in what smelled like rancid cooking oil. Two-thirds of all visible flesh covered in ink. Hard rheumy eyeballs sliding around in skulls. Aggro men with swollen muscles and striated forearms moving like gorillas through the crowd.

Ainsley sighed. The Miami nightclub scene was the final resting place of many well-intentioned illusions about the dating market.

She scanned the crowd for the Legal Weasel. He should

be easy to spot: he looked professional, no visible tattoos. He was an ordinary white guy.

Ainsley did a lap through the nightclub, counting nearly two hundred people—and it was still early. He was nowhere to be seen.

Paul came over with two bottles of beer in his hand. He was wearing a skin-tight white t-shirt that showed off his upper body. Ainsley studiously avoided looking at him.

"So," he said, "my friends will be here soon."

Ainsley swigged her beer. "I didn't know you were inviting people to join us."

"I have to ask you for permission?"

"No," she said, "but you could've let me know."

"I'm doing it now."

"Okay. I'm going to the bathroom."

"All right, have fun."

"I will."

Ainsley handed him her beer to hold, then sashayed over to the bathroom. She felt people's eyes upon her. It was exciting and dangerous at the same time. It'd been a hot minute since she'd been in a place like this. Mostly she and the Legal Weasel had stayed in professional environments.

———

In the bathroom, she used the toilet and came out to wash her hands in the sink. A pair of young women, twenty-one years old, were hitting the metal tampon dispenser on the wall.

"Stop it, Kaylee—"

"But it could work—"

"Wait, don't—"

"Sydney, what the fuck—"

Ainsley washed her hands and dried them with a paper

towel. The girls were normal height and weight but were dressed in clubwear—tight pleather, too much makeup, dyed black hair. One had a tattoo of an unplugged toaster on her thigh. That would be hard to explain.

"Do you need help?" Ainsley asked.

The girls turned around. "This thing ate my money," said the one named Kaylee.

"Do you need a tampon?"

"Yeah, really bad."

"Here, I've got you," said Ainsley. She dug around in her purse and found the extra one that she always carried.

"Oh my God you are the best!" Kaylee said.

"You're welcome," Ainsley replied. "By the way, have either of you seen this guy here tonight?"

Ainsley showed them a photo of the Legal Weasel on her phone. The girls shook their heads. "No, but he's kinda cute."

"Let me know if you see him," said Ainsley.

"Yeah we will," said Sydney.

"Be careful out there," Ainsley added.

But the girls had lost attention and Kaylee disappeared into a stall. Sydney beat on the door. "Hurry up stupid, we need to go outside—"

"Go on the dance floor without me—"

"Nooo—"

Ainsley left the bathroom with a smile on her face. They were less than a decade apart but lived on different planets. Losing her father before high school had done a number on her emotional state. Ainsley didn't want to unpack what exactly that meant, but all she knew was that it'd changed her.

———

Back in the club, Ainsley found Paul standing with a pair of guys in skin-tight muscle t-shirts. All three matched one another.

The two uninvited friends had arrived.

Both had heavily developed muscles. One had shaved his facial hair into a thin black chinstrap beard. He also wore a pair of small round sunglasses, which he peered over the tops of for effect. The other wore a black sequined baseball cap with the word BALLER in a horror monster font. A chaw of tobacco insouciantly bulged from his left cheek.

Ainsley quietly stood alongside them. The trio faced one another but their eyes swept the dance club, looking for targets.

"Not a lotta talent here—"

"I dunno, maybe that one—"

"Naw, she got fucked-up tits—"

"Not that one, the *other* one—"

"Lobster face?"

"Yeah she's a one-and-done—"

"That's a walking STD farm brah—"

"So what, there's shots for that—"

Ainsley cleared her throat. Paul noticed her. "Hey Ainsley, sorry but we drank your beer."

"It wasn't much of a gift anyways," she said. "Who're these guys?"

"Dylan and Lucas," Paul said.

"Hey," said Ainsley. "Does it matter which one of you is which, or can I just call you number one and two?"

"Whoa," said the chinstrap, "this one makes jokes."

"I'm the newest model of clubgirl," Ainsley shot back. "I have a mental processing unit preinstalled. It's called a brain."

"You're not a model," said sequined baseball cap.

Ainsley patted his arm. "It was a joke, man. I'm comparing women to kitchen appliances to make you laugh."

The sequined baseball cap drank his beer and said nothing. Both men made zero eye contact with her. She decided to roll with it for a bit.

"On the prowl," she said. "I get it. It's been a long time. I'm separated."

"Divorced chicks are horny," said the chinstrap.

"Not yet. You have to get me white girl wasted first. Maybe you'll want me then, but it'll be too late."

They didn't laugh at that either. Her quips were arrows whizzing past their target.

Paul said, "Ainsley's here looking for her husband."

"Have you seen him?" said Ainsley. She showed them the same photo she'd shown Kaylee and Sydney in the bathroom.

The duo's eyes flicked down to her screen for the briefest of seconds. "Nope," said one.

"Let me know if you see him. If you're able to rip your eyeballs away from all the tits, of course."

"You should check the VIP room," said the chinstrap.

"Where is it?"

The chinstrap beard nodded towards a corner of the room. A large bouncer in a black polo shirt sat hunched over on a stool, an earpiece in his ear. No line awaited the room.

"Don't respect too many women while I'm gone," she said.

CHAPTER FIFTEEN

Ainsley approached the bouncer outside of the VIP room. He was wider than he was tall. His hair was in tight cornrows and he seemed deep in thought.

"I'm looking for my husband," she said. "Is he here?"

His eyes scanned her up and down. "Do I look like a psychic?"

"That could go either way. They're hard to identify by sight."

"Who are you?"

"Just a helpless girl." She dandled one foot behind the other. A finger found its way to her lip.

"I can't let you in," he said.

She dropped the helpless act. "At least tell me if you've seen this man," she said. Ainsley showed him the photo on her phone.

The bouncer took his time studying the photo of the Legal Weasel. Then he looked up. "What answer do you want to hear?"

"Try a few and let me see which one I like."

"I could say that I've never seen him before. I could also say I let him past this rope an hour ago."

"Which is it?" she said.

"It depends. What's the nature of the problem between you two?"

Just Ainsley's luck. She'd found a bouncer who was so bored that he'd decided to moonlight as a relationship counselor.

"He disappeared on me," she said, "so now I've tracked him here."

The bouncer laid a thoughtful finger against his lips. "So you're hunting for your husband."

"I'm hunting for my wedding ring, and I think he stole it."

A wise look came into the bouncer's eyes. "Are you really looking for the ring? Or something more?"

Now he'd become a guru on a mountaintop. "You know how to ask the tough questions," she said.

He shrugged. "I size people up. It's my job."

"So what's the verdict here?"

He pinched the bridge of his nose between two fingers. "You put me in a dilemma. See, I get paid to screen people. I select the beautiful, the wealthy. But another part of me wants to help people with problems, people like you. That's a good thing, too. You know what I'm saying?

"Yeah, I do."

The man stood up and paced behind his stool. "To resolve this dilemma, I need to betray part of myself. A small death, so that the rest of me may live, and perhaps even be transformed." The bouncer looked up at her with pain in his eyes. "Do you understand? This is existential."

Ainsley shifted her weight but remained patient. She'd sent this man barreling into a serious dark night of the soul.

"You know, I can come back—"

He lifted a hand. "No, these are things I have work

through. I can't run away from big questions." He paused, then exhaled. He dropped his face to his chest. "I'm gonna let you in."

"That decision really took a lot out of you," she said.

"It did."

"Has anyone ever told you that you think too much about your job?"

His eyes searched the ceiling. "No, they haven't."

"Well, you do."

He unhooked the velvet rope from the stanchion. Ainsley pressed her hands together and bowed slightly to him as she passed into the VIP section.

———

She moved around a bend in the hallway, the walls lit in deep pinks and blues. The loud Miami bass of the main room disappeared, replaced by a quieter, muted thudding.

Ainsley curved around a second bend and stopped.

She found herself in an outdoor lounge, open to the stars. Three gas-powered firepits rested in the middle of the stones. Plush stools were arranged against the walls. A lone female bartender waited behind a glass-topped bar.

The room was empty.

"What the hell," she said.

Ainsley headed across the tiles to the bar. "I'm looking for a man," she said. "Have you seen him?"

She flashed the photo on her phone screen.

"Sorry," the woman said, "never seen him before."

"Maybe he came in earlier tonight?" said Ainsley.

"You're our first VIP," came the reply.

Ainsley went back out to the VIP entrance. The bouncer sat on his stool.

"Excuse me," she said.

He ignored her. "You like philosophy?"

"No."

"Me neither."

"The VIP room is empty," she replied. "You could've just told me that."

"People need to discover things for themselves," he said.

———

Ainsley made another circuit through the main room of the club, scanning for her estranged husband.

As the hour had grown later, even more odd creatures had crawled into its dark recesses. A bachelorette party was beating their drunken palms against a security guard's chest. On the dance floor, single men were standing in loose circles shuffled their feet lethargically to a bass-heavy dance beat. Women stood around in Lycra pants that were stretched to the absolute limit of the fabric, their eyelids smeared with enough black mascara to look like it'd been applied with a butter knife.

The Legal Weasel was nowhere to be found.

Ainsley circled back to the last place that she'd seen Paul and his two scuzzy friends, but they'd disappeared. In her sternum, she felt the thudding of the Miami bass. The heat slithered around her face and licked her eyes and ears like dragon's breath.

Then a group on the dance floor caught her eye. They looked familiar.

She edged over to the railing and squinted. It was Kaylee and Sydney, the two girls from the bathroom. They were facing one another as two men attempted to grind on them from behind.

Ainsley squinted harder. The two men looked familiar too.

It was chinstrap beard and sequined baseball cap.

Their hands were all over the young girls. Kaylee pushed chinstrap away, but he came right back. Sydney was ignoring sequined baseball cap in the hopes that he might disappear. They were too young, or too drunk to put up resistance.

At this moment, Ainsley had never felt older. Not even thirty, and she could see the two younger women hurtling towards the cliff's edge. Usually in a group of girls at the club, there was a responsible one. One to hold the others' hair back in the toilet, gather up the purses, call for the ride.

These two didn't have anybody like that.

She weighed her options. Ainsley could ignore the scene and go about her business and let the girls get chewed up by the creepy critters of the nightlife scene. Or she could do some good and save the girls the trouble of filing a police report or receiving penicillin injections.

Ainsley squinched up her face. This was decision time.

She knew the answer. She'd try to do some good.

She walked over to one of the bars and bought three lemon drop shots. Then Ainsley hightailed it to the dance floor, holding them in the air, mouth open. She was giving the impression of having the time of her life.

Chinstrap and sequined baseball cap had now separated the girls. They were each gorilla dancing, their large torsos curving around and dwarfing the girls. Their faces were in the girls' ears whispering who-knows-what.

"Kaylee and Sydney!" shouted Ainsley. "Oh my god, I've been looking for you!" She showed them the shots. "Take one!"

The young girls' eyes lit up. They disengaged from the two men and joined Ainsley.

"For real?" said Sydney.

"Yeah!" said Ainsley.

"To tampons and cheap shots!" shouted Ainsley.

"Whoo!" the girls screamed in unison.

All three women threw the shots backwards down their throats. Chinstrap and sequined baseball cap circled around the trio, visibly annoyed.

"You're the best club mom ever!" said Kaylee.

"I don't know if that's a compliment but thank you!" shouted Ainsley. "Now bring yourselves in closer. I have to tell you something else."

She put her arms across the young girls' shoulders. The three brought their heads together until they were almost touching.

"Do you know these guys?" Ainsley said.

"We, like, just met them," said Sydney.

"These are the type of guys that will screw up your life."

"But they're cute—" said Kaylee.

"It doesn't matter," said Ainsley. "I know a friend of theirs. Trust me, you don't want anything to do with them."

The two girls were staring at her with glassy eyes. She got the sense that they hadn't really processed what she'd just said.

"Do you understand?"

"Yeah," said Kaylee.

"Don't waste any time on them."

"I told you they were gross—" said Sydney.

"Whatever," said Kaylee. She turned back to chinstrap. Ainsley grabbed her arm and yanked her back.

"What's your problem?" shouted chinstrap. He pushed Ainsley in the shoulder, sending her backwards two steps. He stood over her, glowering and menacing. "You hag. Nobody wants to look at you!"

Ainsley recovered herself, held up her palms. "There's no problem," she said, slowly backing away. "I'm out. Have a great night."

Paul caught her on her way out of the club. "What did you say to my friends?"

"I saved a couple girls from making a bad decision."

"You cockblocked my boys."

Ainsley put a hand on her hip. "You are the first Ph.D. candidate I've ever heard use that word."

He gestured around the club. "Look at the people here. What do you see?"

"A lot of douchebags," replied Ainsley.

Paul looked at her. "What are you trying to say?"

"You used to be different," she said.

"How so?" he said.

"You know what I'm trying to say."

"No, tell me."

"Paul, you used to be more real. You talked about books and movies and the world."

Paul grew animated. "Ainsley, I was poor. People used me. I let myself be used. I was romantic. I overthought too much." A trio of young women giggled by. Paul's head swiveled and his eyes followed them. "Now I'm a man of action."

"How old are you?"

"Thirty-eight."

"So you're not so young anymore."

"Neither are you."

"I'm twenty-nine," she shot back. "And I don't care about your judgment. I just need to find my husband. You volunteered to help me. Remember?"

He smirked. "Yeah, I remember."

Ainsley patted him on the chest. "I don't think Miami changed you. I think you changed yourself."

She walked out of the nightclub.

CHAPTER SIXTEEN

A quarter to noon.

Ainsley lay in her hotel bed, watching huge-eyed CGI characters bop across the television screen. It was a Saturday morning cartoon meant for preschoolers.

She looked at her phone again, out of habit. The average person did it forty-three times a day. Nothing. She set it down again. Wayne had messaged earlier in the morning that Jared's location wasn't showing up any longer, but Ainsley knew that could be anything. He could've shut off the phone or put it on airplane mode.

Since then, no messages, no emails. Nobody in the world wanted Ainsley for anything. Thousands of ways to communicate, and fewer reasons to talk to other people than ever before.

A knock at the door. "Room service," said a muffled voice.

She'd ordered food over an hour ago. Ainsley stood, wrapped a robe around herself, and opened the door. A young Cuban guy with a narrow face walked guiltily into the room. "*Aqui?*" he said, standing over her table.

"*Esta bien,*" Ainsley replied.

He set down the tray. "*Que los deje fuera despues*."

"*Claro que si*."

He paused, glanced at her. "*Que bien tu español*."

"*Gracias*."

The door closed behind him, and she shut off the television and sat at the small table, scarfing down the French toast and the coffee. Her Spanish really wasn't that good—all she'd said was *it's good* and *of course*—but the bar was low for white Americans.

Regardless, Ainsley had the three things needed to acquire a foreign language: a good listening ear, a need to talk, and a fearless disregard for her own mistakes.

When she'd finished, she flopped back on the bed. This purposelessness was no fun. It was exactly what she shouldn't be doing at this time in her life. She needed to stay active, to layer more slices of life between her current self and her past self.

She pulled herself up to a sitting position. This was Miami. She would take advantage of it.

————

She'd spent the afternoon strolling around the Vizcaya Museum and Gardens. It was a Coconut Grove mansion constructed in the 1920s by a wealthy agricultural industrialist—James Deering, who'd built and sold harvesters. They said he'd enjoyed pulling up to the dock on his mansion in his yacht. He'd been a conservationist too, preserving all the mangrove swamps and tropical forests.

Now the mangroves were mostly gone, and everybody knew the ocean was rising higher every year. Miami already flooded frequently, and it was estimated to rise to 60 days a year by the middle of the twenty-first century.

South Florida's past was going to be very different from its future.

Then Ainsley had headed to Coral Gables, where the heavy branches of the tropical trees were laden with Spanish moss like gold bracelets hanging from the forearms of a gypsy. She'd seated herself at a sidewalk table at a high-end restaurant. Behind her, through the open doorway of the restaurant, waiters in white shirts and black pants shuttled small plates of food out of the kitchen. The aroma of seafood, herbs, and olive oil floated through the air into her nostrils.

She ordered a glass of white wine and settled back to watch the passersby. Ainsley had been a people watcher since she was old enough to remember. She'd been an only child, so making up stories about people, or reading books about made-up people, had been her biggest pastimes.

A waiter arrived at her table. He was holding a small plate of seared shrimp in olive oil, accompanied by a side of toasted ciabatta.

He gently slid the plate before her. "Courtesy of the man at the bar."

Ainsley whipped her head around. At the bar sat a very attractive man with a silver beard and a head of silver hair. He was too old for her for sure—he had to be at least forty—but he was dressed well and his grooming was on point.

Plus, that beard. Ainsley had always found them attractive. Too bad this was the wrong time.

"No thank you," she said.

The waiter nodded slightly, as though he'd expected that answer. Then he carried the plate back to the kitchen.

A moment later, Ainsley was aware of a presence standing to her right. She looked over. The man from the bar was standing there, holding the plate.

"You don't have to talk to me, but please don't reject food from this kitchen. It's one of the best in the city."

Instinctively, Ainsley sat up. He courteously slid it in front of her. "To be honest, it's good that you rejected it, because it would've been too hot. It's cooler now."

"I'm glad you know what's best for me," she said.

"I know that you're either separated, or wishing that you were," he retorted.

Ainsley's mouth dropped open. "How do you know that?"

"There's a tan line on your ring finger," he said.

She glanced down. There was the proof. She'd incurred that by spending most of her waking moments at the beach last summer.

Before she could protest, he'd pulled out the other chair at her table and sat down, angling his body so that he too faced the sidewalk.

"Go on," he said, "I won't watch. I'll just entertain you with stories about everybody who passes by."

Ainsley felt herself being drawn into his net. She didn't complain. What else was she doing tonight?

"That guy has four grown children who won't return his calls. That old lady runs the donation box at her church but harbors a terrible secret about her first boyfriend who died in a tragic diving accident. And that guy clobbers his wife. Look at how he holds his arms."

As he went on, Ainsley was only half-listening to him. The shrimp was that spectacular. It occupied most of her thoughts.

"What are you doing in Miami?" she said.

"Business," he replied. "I'm here for a couple of weeks while my Florida partners try to weasel out of our contract."

"I take it they won't."

He shook his head. "They've got too much exposure. They're mine."

The man caught her eyes. She understood the subtext.

"I'm Ainsley," she said.

"Pierre," he replied.

"You're French?"

"My parents were. I went to boarding school in the Dordogne but that's it. I've lived mostly in New York. You?"

"Nowhere. I live in a place that has no significance to me."

"Well, that's sad."

"I think a lot of people feel the same nowadays."

"You could move."

"I've thought about it," said Ainsley, "but I wouldn't know where. Mostly I just want to travel. I want to see the world."

"Oh, you should," he said. "I traveled with my ex-wife for almost five years. I learned a lot."

"Like what?"

"Always travel with a silicon spatula. You can't find them abroad and there's no better way to make eggs in the morning."

She laughed, covering her mouth. It erupted out of her with no warning and surprised her. It was the first genuine laugh she'd felt in months.

CHAPTER SEVENTEEN

Three hours later, Ainsley was making out with Pierre in a darkened corner of a public park. His beard was soft and his lips felt like firm but gentle cushions. This man knew how to kiss.

They'd bounced to a second location, a bar, where Ainsley had ordered a French 75 and told him that it was in honor of both his heritage and his age. He'd taken the joke in stride.

Her head swimming with the alcohol, they'd walked down the street until he'd pulled her into this darkened park. Now Pierre's hands were all over her back, from fluttering the delicate points of her shoulder blades to caressing the curve of her waist to cupping the small mounds of her buttocks. Ainsley wasn't resisting either. His body felt just as good. He wasn't tall but he was lean and functionally strong. He had the type of sinewy muscles that could carry him to the top of a tree or swim to a distant island.

Ainsley knew where this was going, but she couldn't stop it. She didn't want to stop it. She only hoped that she'd have a chance to snap a photo of Pierre's ID and send it to Deirdre, just in case.

She was in a bad place, making bad choices, but it was expected. She needed to give herself permission to get through this period.

"I'm staying right down the street," he murmured, his face buried in her throat.

"Where at?" she gasped.

"The Biltmore."

"How fancy."

"It's old."

"Then it fits you," she answered.

He grabbed the hair at the back of her head. "You have a smart mouth."

"It graduated at the top of its class." She let out a giggle.

"Let's go."

He released her hair, grasped her hand, and pulled her out of the park and down the sidewalk towards his hotel.

———

Ainsley's head hit the pillow, and Pierre's body was on top of hers an instant later. His shirt was already off and his face was upon her own.

Then she remembered something.

"Pierre," she said, turning her face to the side, pushing his shoulders back gently, "can you hold on just a minute?"

He paused, lifted his head. "What is it?"

"I have to set an alarm."

"Why?"

"Because I don't want to fall asleep here."

Pierre shrugged and rolled off her. Ainsley stood up from the bed and went to her white bag and pulled out her phone. It was nine o'clock. She was going to set an alarm for midnight. That was enough time to enjoy one another.

She slid open her phone. A message was waiting from Wayne, sent nearly three hours ago.

You'll never guess where he is now. Robin's out so you can call me.

She glanced back at Pierre. He was laying on the bed, shirtless, looking at her with a hungry look in his eye.

"I need to make a phone call," she said. "I'm really sorry."

He gestured to the bathroom. She gave him an apologetic smile.

The bathroom was small and old. A claw-footed bathtub with an old-fashioned spigot sat opposite the low toilet. A single light fixture above the mirror hadn't been changed in well over half a century.

Ainsley perched herself on the edge of the tub and dialed Wayne. He picked up on the second ring.

"What took you so long?" he said.

"I got sidetracked."

"By what?"

"A guy."

"You don't waste any time, do you?"

"Just tell me where he is."

Her brother-in-law chuckled. "The reason I couldn't track him for most of the day was that he was evidently on an airplane."

"To where?"

"Paso Robles, California."

"I've never heard of it," Ainsley said.

"It's wine country. I've traced his location to a winery and inn called La Marmota Vineyards."

Her head was spinning, and it wasn't from the French 75. "Jared doesn't even drink wine. He's a beer guy."

"That's what I said. But nonetheless, he's there. I even called the front desk to find out how long he would be staying. I told them that I wanted to send him a complimentary dinner for tomorrow night. They informed me that he was checking out tomorrow."

Ainsley chewed on her lip. Through the sliver of the bathroom door, she could see Pierre reclining on the bed, inspecting a fingernail.

"Ainsley?" Wayne said.

"I'm thinking," she replied, a bit too sharply.

"You could make it. It's a four-hour flight from Miami but with the three-hour time difference, you'd land one hour after you leave. Leave Miami on a nine o'clock am flight and you're there at ten o'clock am California time."

"I have to do it," she said.

"If you find him, you'll have to come up with an amazing cover story."

Her mind was racing. She'd have to go now, buy a ticket immediately, run back to her hotel, pack like the wind. It depended on the time of the flight that she could find.

"Thanks," she said.

"I'm rooting for you," he replied. "I'll text you the address."

They disconnected. Ainsley tapped her foot. In the space of two minutes, her entire mentality had refocused itself upon the mission at hand.

Not on Pierre.

She slowly stood up, her shoulders stooped slightly. Ainsley re-entered the bedroom. He grinned as she came back into sight.

"Everything all right?"

She exhaled. "No."

"Why?"

"I got some news and unfortunately I have to go."

"Like, right this minute?"

Ainsley nodded sadly. "It's not you. I'm chasing my ex-husband to get my ring back. I just found out that he's in

California." She paused. "I'm not as crazy as I sound, please believe me."

Pierre's eyes widened. "You didn't seem like a bunny boiler."

"It's a long story," she said, collecting her purse and her coat. "I'd love to tell you about it some other time."

He was already on his feet and pulling his shirt back on. "Let's be honest. There won't be another time."

Pierre opened the hotel room door and gestured for her to leave. Embarrassed, Ainsley hung her head as she moved past him. He put his arm out across the doorway, stopping her. She lifted her face towards his.

He kissed her deeply. "Good luck finding him, Ainsley."

She mustered a poor imitation of a smile, then left, feeling horrible.

PASO ROBLES

CHAPTER EIGHTEEN

The rental Audi felt powerful beneath Ainsley's hands as she twisted through the winding country roads.

She'd booked a seven am flight from Miami. A quick connection in Los Angeles, and she'd found herself at the San Luis Obispo airport, thirty miles south of Paso Robles, at eight-thirty am. She'd walked up to the counter and rented this car.

Now it was nine-thirty, and she'd shut off her GPS. Ainsley had never liked disembodied voices telling her when to turn or where to go. Instead, she scanned the signs on the sides of the road. *Minassian-Young Winery, 3 miles*. That was how people navigated the rolling hills around here.

Tall valley oaks arched over the country lane, their branches forming a canopy over the road. Yellow sunlight dappled on the black asphalt. To the right, rows of neatly manicured red-and-green grapevines flashed past. Then a driveway marked the entrance to the winery, which was called Opolo Vineyards.

Ainsley passed it. La Marmota was situated further out, on

the far western edge of the viticultural area. She passed an olive oil press, some rustic fruit stands, another winery named Justin. She recognized that name from the wine aisle at her grocery store. She'd spent a little too much time there in recent weeks.

Nervous about the time, she accelerated slightly. The Audi went around a sharp bend, lurched down a sudden dip, and then screamed to a halt.

La Marmota loomed before her, on the left. It was snuggled up underneath a tall ridgeline, with grapes planted all the way up to the rock wall. The sign gave every indication of expense, its cursive copper script stamped against a granite slab. To the right of the words was the outline of a small rodent.

That was the marmot.

She pulled into the property and parked her car in the gravel lot.

Ainsley stepped out of the car and inhaled. The air here was sweet and lush and ripe. For a moment, she wondered why the United States had earned such a bad reputation abroad. If foreign visitors ever came to this part of the country, they'd never want to leave.

A sign pointed towards the tasting room. Another sign pointed towards the inn.

"I'm here, you bastard," she said to nobody.

She slung her bag across her shoulder and walked up towards the inn.

———

The Inn at La Marmota was a large California Mexican-style ranch. It was new and pristine, a vision in ochre stucco that promised luxurious respite from the dangerous fields of wine that surrounded the property. The inn boasted twelve rooms tucked in and around the fancy courtyard with a tinkling fountain and hanging succulents.

Ainsley stepped into the small welcome lobby. It was decorated as perfectly as a movie set. White couches with chenille throws. A stack of coffee table books positioned just so. A crystal decanter of white lilies in the sunlit window.

And a marmot.

The small creature was in a metal cage on a rustic table against a wall. It was hunched into a small ball in its bed of woodchips. On the cage hung a hand-printed wooden sign that read *I am cute, but please don't touch me.*

"That's Jerry," said a woman's voice.

Ainsley turned. Behind a free-standing mahogany desk with thin legs waited a middle-aged woman, looking at her over the tops of her glasses. An open laptop and some documents rounded out the appearance of work.

"He's a cutie," said Ainsley.

"Can I help you with something?" the woman said.

"I was wondering if you have a room available tonight," said Ainsley.

"I believe we do," said the woman, shifting to her laptop screen. "Yes, we have a couple checking out."

"When did they check in?" Ainsley blurted.

"Oh, I'm afraid I can't tell you that," the woman said.

"Sorry," said Ainsley. "I don't know why I asked that."

"If you'd like to give me your information, we can get you all set up."

Ainsley handed over her ID and, reluctantly, her credit card. "Is there a breakfast available this morning?"

The woman's eyes stayed fixed on her screen. "There was, but it was only for guests who stayed the night. It's almost finished anyways."

"Where is it located?"

"On our dining patio." She looked up. "If you're hungry, there's a farmhouse stand down the road that opens at noon."

"Thanks."

Ainsley went over to the marmot cage and crouched down and looked at the sleeping rodent. Next to the cage she saw a short stack of old copies of *Wine Spectator* magazine. She remembered seeing one of those in the Legal Weasel's box of items from his office.

"What are you visiting Paso Robles for?" the woman said.

"The usual."

"Wine."

"Yep."

"You're traveling alone?"

Ainsley thought quickly. "I'm meeting friends later, for a bachelorette party. I was invited last minute and their hotel was full."

The woman said, "I see. Well, please don't bring them here. We have a policy against bachelorette parties."

"They're staying downtown."

"Oh, very nice. Please sign here, Ainsley. Your room will be ready at three."

Ainsley took the pen and scrawled her signature. "I think I'm going to explore the property."

"Delightful," said the woman. "My name is Diane, if you need anything. Our tasting room opens at noon as well."

———

Eleven o'clock am, checkout time.

Ainsley had positioned herself in an iron deck chair at the edge of the nearest courtyard. A single floral cushion had been placed on the seat, but her back rested on the uncomfortable grillwork.

She'd chosen this vantage point on purpose. All guests

needed to walk past her to get to the registration area and the parking lot.

If this was a game of chess, she'd forced checkmate—though perhaps *former mate* would be better.

Ainsley held a cup of coffee, filched from the dining room, and enjoyed the sun on her face. She listened to the rustling of the trees. She studied the grapes slowly bulging on the vines.

What would she do when the Legal Weasel finally saw her?

She had a lot of options. She could play it angry. She could play it cool. She could play it friendly. She could play it lots of ways.

That was the entire problem, in fact. Ainsley was a welter of conflicting emotions and didn't know which one to follow. She was a mess, but honestly it would be more worrisome if she *weren't* a mess. Only a psychopath could've cruised serenely through the emotional chaos of the last two months of her life.

She tapped her foot. At the very least, she'd have to explain how she'd tracked him here, without giving up his brother-in-law. It would have to be his law firm. A colleague had seen him looking at Miami hotels on his phone. Ainsley could take a flyer and guess that he'd also been looking at Paso Robles winery inns. That approach could backfire.

Maybe she could take a different tack and explain that she'd placed a tracker on his luggage. In hindsight, that would've been a brilliant idea, if she'd thought of it. But doing so would've meant that she'd suspected he was going to leave her, in advance—and she hadn't. The empty apartment had walloped her like a roundhouse from a heavyweight.

But mostly, she reminded herself, she wasn't here to see him, or whatever floozy he'd picked up. She'd tracked him across the country in order to recover her stolen engagement ring.

Wasn't that the reason?

Ainsley heard the voices of a couple approaching. The sound of rolling suitcases accompanied them. Her body tensed. She sat up in her chair, crossed her legs carefully, passed a hand through her hair.

As the couple passed her chair, Ainsley summoned the courage to look at them.

It wasn't the Legal Weasel. It was an older couple, tanned and athletic. The man was dressed in a blue polo shirt and ironed chinos, his wife in a flowing white one-piece dress with sandals. Each had sunglasses parked on top of their hairline. They looked like the epitome of Southern California wealth and health.

"Did you hear when they started up again at three o'clock—"

"They were so loud—"

"All that shouting, what do you think they were fighting about—"

"I heard him shouting about a ring—"

"Yes, and she didn't care, so it clearly wasn't hers—"

Ainsley felt her heartbeat accelerate. She stood up and quickly concocted an innocent lie. "Excuse me?"

The couple stopped and turned. "Yes?"

"I'm glad I wasn't the only one who was kept awake by that couple last night. Do you know who they were?"

"Goodness, no, but they were right next door to us." She pointed towards room seven.

"Just a dreadful couple," Ainsley agreed.

The woman's eyes went wide. "Can you believe arguing like that in the middle of the night? So loudly! I can't believe it."

"Did you hear what happened with the ring?" said Ainsley.

The husband replied: "He was yelling that he wanted to go back to the winery for it, that he was changing his mind, but she refused."

Ainsley tried to play it cool. What was her husband changing his mind about? Also, it sounded like, if the Legal Weasel had his way, he could be returning to the winery later that day.

"I didn't hear that part," she said. "Which winery was it?"

"Trebuchet," the husband answered. "I heard him say it several times. The woman was disagreeing with him. She just wanted to leave."

"I missed all that," his wife said.

"That was when you were in the bathroom," he said.

"Anyways," his wife said, "we're going to let Diane know what happened so she doesn't allow those guests back. We come here at least twice a year and don't want to run into them again."

Ainsley waved goodbye. "Have a good day. Take a nap!"

"You too!" The couple disappeared into the lobby.

Ainsley was perplexed. Yelling was not something the Legal Weasel ever really did. He was more of a quiet plotter in the background. All their real disagreements had been either faced civilly or just ignored.

Ainsley sat down again and removed a Paso Robles winery map from her purse. She'd taken a copy earlier from the lobby. It was published by the local chamber of commerce.

She ran her finger down the alphabetical listing of wineries on the back side, stopped at the Ts.

There it was. Trebuchet Winery, square G7. She flipped over the map and found it. Trebuchet was situated on the eastern side of the viticultural region. It looked to be about twenty miles away.

Ainsley snapped the map shut and quickly walked over to room seven. The door had been left partly open. She'd been looking at it for the last forty-five minutes, so she was pretty sure what she was going to find.

She knocked on the door, waited. There was no response. She looked inside the room.

It was empty, as expected.

Ainsley slipped inside. The bed was a mess of sheets and comforters. On the bedside table stood an empty canister of Pringles. A smile appeared involuntarily on Ainsley's lips. Those were her husband's favorite. She used to poke fun at him for eating what she called Frankenstein chips, compressed and packed with wheat mulch, oh why couldn't he eat real chips, like Lay's, which were *obviously* better, and sometimes the annoyed tickling would begin—

Those were happier times.

In the bathroom, she found makeup smudges on the hand towels. A discarded green mascara tube was in the trash can. She fished it out, unscrewed it, and pulled out the brush. She didn't know why she did that. It didn't yield any insights into the woman who'd replaced her.

Ainsley waited for feelings of jealousy to arrive. They never came. She felt curiously detached.

"Housekeeping," said a small voice.

Startled, Ainsley stepped back into the room.

"Hi," she said.

"I can come back—"

"No," said Ainsley, "I was leaving anyways."

She quickly slipped past the cleaning woman. Then she went to the parking lot, stepped inside her rental car, started the engine, and pulled out of La Marmota.

She pointed the nose of her Audi to the east.

CHAPTER NINETEEN

The eastern half of Paso Robles was different from the western half of the region. Gone were the oaks, the mountains, the lush greenery, the shade.

Instead, the other side was nothing but hot, rolling plains.

Despite this, the terrain was still blanketed with thousands of acres of grapevines, crisscrossed by gravel roads and dirt paths. Ainsley cranked up the air conditioning in her car and mopped sweat from her forehead. She didn't know how any fruit could survive in this environment, no matter how tiny.

She followed the winery signs, deeper into the fields, until the town of Paso Robles was a memory in the rearview.

Then she saw it.

Trebuchet Vineyards. It was plunked in the middle of nowhere.

Ainsley parked the car and stepped out and took in the scene. The small winery had stone walls, a heavy wooden door, a patio with a few tables beneath umbrellas. Behind the customer tasting area stood the real operation—huge tanks, presses, filters on caster wheels, stacks of oak barrels—all stored under a high roof. A pair of Mexican workers in jeans and boots and neckerchiefs were hosing off some equipment.

Ainsley pursed her lips, thinking. Was it worth it to set up a fake story? She decided there wasn't. She would be direct.

She walked through the blinding heat to the heavy door. A small sign read *Tasting Room*. She pulled it open.

The room resembled an English pub. Down one side ran a short wooden counter with six battered stools. Dark wooden walls on four sides that showed their age, a single small window cut into the far end. The black slate floor was uneven and pocked with damage from chair legs.

A sign above the bar read: *Trebuchet Vineyards, founded 1978*. Another sign offered a twenty-five percent discount if you signed up for the wine club.

There were only three other people in the room: a young couple doing a romantic tasting on a pair of stools, and a blonde woman about Ainsley's age standing behind the bar, an apron around her waist. On the counter, a row of uncorked Trebuchet wine bottles awaited duty.

"Welcome to Trebuchet," said the woman cheerfully, "how ya doin?"

"Not bad," replied Ainsley.

"You here for a tasting?"

"Sure."

Ainsley pulled up a stool. The woman produced a piece of clean stemware and placed it before her. "First we're going to start with the whites." Then she removed the first bottle from the lineup and tipped it into the glass, pouring an ounce. "This is our Sauvignon Blanc, estate grown and casked, about nine percent alcohol, with notes of lemon and lilac. Be sure to swirl it so it opens up."

Ainsley put her fingers around the base and gently shook the glass so the liquid sloshed around. Then she lifted it to her lips and drank. It was sweet, floral, and citric all at once.

"That's lovely," she said.

"It's one of our two flagship varietals, along with the cab. My name is Trish, by the way."

"I'm Ainsley."

Trish went down the counter to the other couple, who were already on the reds. Ainsley watched her pour them the merlot, explaining something about the elevation of the vineyards. Through the window, she saw the two Mexican guys rolling metal equipment across the bay.

Then Trish came back. "You ready for the next one?"

"I have a question first."

The woman nodded. "Hit me."

"I need to know if a certain man came into this tasting room yesterday."

Trish looked alarmed. "I wasn't here yesterday. My son was sick. Who are you looking for?"

Ainsley decided to show her cards. "My husband." She lowered her voice: "He's with another woman."

Trish's eyes flashed with surprise. Drama had been revealed, and Ainsley now sensed that she had an ally.

"Shit. Are you a detective or something?"

Ainsley shook her head. "Not yet, but I'm starting to feel like one."

"Bruce was working the counter yesterday. He's the owner." She paused. "He's also my dad."

"Can I talk to him?"

"You can try," she said. Her eyes told a different story.

That was a mysterious response. Ainsley would soon understand what she meant, for the back door of the tasting room flew open, and Bruce Falston burst into the room.

———

Ainsley stared at the old man. He was built like a bear, a prodigious round belly flopping over his belt. His ripped white t-shirt was stained purple with sloppy wine., Scruffy white stubble and mussed short white hair completed the picture.

Even more, the wild look in his eyes told Ainsley that Bruce Falston wasn't your typical senior citizen.

"Who wants a tour of my cellars?" he bellowed.

The couple at the end of the counter froze. Nobody replied.

Ainsley lifted a hand. "I do."

He cranked his arm in a come-over motion. "Then get your sweet little butts back here!"

Trish exchanged looks with Ainsley. *You asked for it.*

Ainsley went over to the back cellar door. Bruce turned to his daughter. "You seen Fernando today?"

"Nope," said Trish.

"He didn't call in?"

"Nope."

"That son of a bitch." He turned to the couple. "Get off those stools and come get yourselves edjumacated. You won't get another offer like this at any other winery, that's guaranteed."

"There's cellar tours all over the region," said the guy.

Bruce's face went purple. He went over and yanked their glasses away from them. "This is my life's work, you idiot. Now follow me and learn something."

He stared at them in the eyes. Chastised, the couple exchanged looks, then stood up and followed Ainsley and the madman into the wine cellar.

CHAPTER TWENTY

Trebuchet didn't have a cellar by definition, since few structures in California had basements. But it did have a long, dark room whose stone walls kept it quite a bit chillier than the surrounding hot fields. So did the portable free-standing AC units placed at strategic intervals along the floor.

Bruce Falston strode proudly through the rows of barrels. "We maintain a nice fifty-five degrees in here. That's the temperature that my lovelies like to stay at." He patted a barrel, then looked back at his three guests. "You don't measure in Celsius, like some of my other visitors, do ya?"

Ainsley shook her head no. "Fahrenheit is better. It's more precise."

Bruce's eyes lit up. "Yes! Finally, someone understands! I get in so many fights with so many Europeans about that." He swung a beefy arm across Ainsley's shoulder. "Oh, I can tell that we're gonna get along. We gonna have a good time! Ha!"

Ainsley sniffed. The winemaker smelled of ripe grapes and even riper sweat. It wasn't a completely terrible mixture.

He continued walking until he stopped at a barrel, planted

a hand on it, and turned to face them. "You haven't tasted a cab until you've tasted this one."

Bruce tilted his head. "Did you just roll your eyes at me?"

He was looking at the couple again. They froze. Ainsley hadn't been looking at them.

"No," said the young man.

"I think you did."

"Listen, Bruce, it's just that—"

"That's Mister Falston to you."

"Sorry, Mister Falston, I mean, there's a lot of good cabernet sauvignon out here—"

The winemaker tightened his mouth. "It's because I don't win awards, isn't it?"

"I don't know how many awards you win—"

The old winemaker's fists clenched. "You know why I don't win those awards? They won't *let* me win! They don't like me! I don't play their games, kiss the right asses, go to the right festivals. I'm just out here in the fields, on my own, me and Trish and the three laborers. Those prizes can go to hell. My wine is better than all of theirs. Here, I'll prove it."

He used the tip of a knife to pry out the stopper of the barrel. Then he produced what looked like a large glass eyedropper and slid it into the hole. His fingers squeezed the rubber ball at one end and slowly released the squeeze, drawing the wine into the dropper.

Then Bruce withdrew the small instrument. It had filled almost entirely with an inky purple-red liquid.

"This is my cabernet sauvignon. Barreled three years ago, it's almost ready to bottle."

He walked over to Ainsley and lifted it into the air above her head. "Open your mouth."

Ainsley tilted her head back and opened her mouth. He squeezed the dropper and sent a stream of purple wine into the back of her throat.

He lowered the instrument. "Don't swallow it yet," he said. "Just gently roll that around your mouth for a while and savor it. See what flavors you find."

Ainsley did as he instructed. The liquid was heavy, almost chewy, in her mouth. It tasted like blackberry and cherry and other fruits. When she finally swallowed, it left a taste of leather on her tongue.

"That's what we call a California fruit bomb," Bruce said. "Whaddya think?"

"It's honestly amazing." That was the truth.

"Of course it's amazing. It should've taken over the world by now but I can only make about eight hundred cases a year. We're limited by the vines. I can't find enough grapes of this quality."

Bruce went over to the other couple and held the dropper above the young man's face. "Open up."

The young man rolled his eyes again, then tilted his head up and opened his mouth. Bruce angled the dropper to the left and squirted the wine onto his shoulder. "Oops, sorry about that. Hope that shirt wasn't expensive. Lemme try again."

———

The tour carried on, Bruce passionately explaining the world of wine production. He explained how grapes in hot climates produced the best wine. "They *like* being tortured," he said, "so I torture them."

To explain the effect of the type of wood upon the aging process, he shoved Ainsley's head into two different barrels, one made of French oak and the other American oak. She pretended she could smell the difference.

He talked about the level of alcohol in the wines. By law, producers were restricted to fourteen percent, because anything higher than that would mean landing in a different tax bracket. As a result, he said, many winemakers lied on their labels—and you can tell if they lied when a scorching feeling runs down your esophagus after drinking what is supposedly an ordinary red.

"It's probably closer to twenty," Bruce said, "and you'd best eat something along with it."

Meanwhile, Ainsley was biding her time, waiting for the right moment.

Then it came.

Bruce had led them to the final cask, a dessert wine he'd been experimenting with. The young man had excused himself to the bathroom to scrub out the stains from the shoulder, and the young woman was toying with her phone.

That left Ainsley alone. The winemaker handed her a small goblet of dessert wine. "The grand finale," he said.

"Bruce, can I ask if you were here yesterday?"

"I'm here every day, my love," he replied.

"Trish told me you might be able to help me. I'm looking for a man who came here for a tasting yesterday."

He shook his head. "You're talking to a man with the memory of a fish. I probably won't remember you in half an hour."

"Can I show you a photo of him?"

"You can try."

Ainsley pulled up a recent photo of the Legal Weasel. She still had piles of them on her phone. She wasn't ready to delete any yet. There would be time to do that later.

"I think I remember him," the winemaker said.

"He was apparently with a woman."

He lifted his index finger. "Yes. I remember her better."

"Why?"

"She was a stunner. They bought two bottles of my old vine grenache."

The old winemaker's memory was better than he'd let on.

"Well," said Ainsley, "that man is my husband."

Bruce's eyebrows shot up. "Well, that changes the conversation, doesn't it?"

"I know."

"You just let him run around with supermodels or what?"

"I don't know who she is and I don't care. We're separated. I only want one thing."

"What's that?"

"My engagement ring. He took it when he left me."

"Good luck with that."

She faced him square on. "I've been told he left it here yesterday."

Bruce lifted an eyebrow. "Really?"

"Yes. Could you ask around?"

"Trish didn't see it because she wasn't here. I didn't see it either. That only leaves our three laborers."

"And their names are—"

"Juan, Diego, and Fernando. They don't speak English."

The first two were the workers she'd seen outside. Fernando hadn't shown up today.

"Could you ask them for me?"

"You want to ask them yourself?"

"Yeah."

"Then let's do it."

Bruce gestured her to follow her outside. Then he looked at the young woman, still toying on her phone. "You two can find your own way out."

CHAPTER TWENTY-ONE

They stepped outside the winery into the brightness and the heat. The men were nowhere to be seen. Bruce placed a hand over his eyes and peered around the fields.

"They're over there," he said, pointing. "They're pruning over in sector fourteen."

Ainsley spotted the two heads in the distance. "Should we walk?"

"There's no other way to get there. I'll introduce you to the grapes!"

Ainsley stepped into the vineyard, following the old man through his vines. His fingers passed along the leaves, lightly touching, humming to himself. This was a total change from his indoors self. This was where he seemed happiest.

"What's the story of these vines?"

"I planted them fifty years ago," he said, "before anybody had discovered this region. They mocked me, but now look who's laughing!" Bruce let out an exaggerated guffaw that echoed across the vineyard.

"Your daughter loves wine the way you do?"

"She'd better! Or I'm cutting her out of the will."

Ainsley knew that with a father like Bruce Falston, it was better to go along with what he wanted. He was a force. Some people are rocks in the stream of life, so headstrong that even the water diverts and passes around them.

They arrived at where the two men were working in the vines. They had donned broad hats and gloves. On the ground between them lay a wide basket of clippings and a small speaker that was playing ranchera music.

"*Manos*," he said. That was short for *hermanos*.

Juan and Diego turned towards him. One wiped his sleeve across his sweaty face.

Bruce spoke to them rapidly in Spanish, with little trace of an American accent. It shouldn't have been a surprise to Ainsley, but it still was. A lifetime of working in the fields of central California probably necessitated it.

The men shook their heads. One said, "*Salió anoche y no nos dijo nada.*"

Ainsley could understand that. *He went out last night and didn't tell us anything.*

Bruce turned to her. "They didn't see a ring, and they don't know where Fernando went."

"Be honest with me," said Ainsley. "Could the two things be connected?"

"Could Fernando have stolen your ring?" Bruce shrugged. "I don't know. He's new."

"How long had he been here?"

"Not even a month. His cousin Renata at the taqueria recommended him to me."

"What about Juan and Diego?"

"They don't know him either. They've been working for me for almost twenty years."

Ainsley moodily kicked at a rock with the toe of her shoe. The two field-hands went back to pruning the grapevines.

"You could buy another ring," Bruce suggested.

"I don't want another ring," she replied. "I just don't like being robbed by my soon-to-be ex-husband. It's humiliating."

"Listen, Ashley——" he said.

"My name is Ainsley."

"——whatever your name is, follow me back to the tasting room. Drinks are on me."

The winemaker put a warm hand on her shoulder. She mustered up a half-smile.

————

Three hours later, Ainsley stumbled out of the tasting room towards her rental car. Her teeth were wine-stained purple and her walk was unsteady.

Bruce had spent the first hour regaling the visitors to the tasting room with stories of a life in the vines. Ainsley had watched the visitors warm up to him in varying degrees. The more fragile ones couldn't handle him, and one couple even fled. Others drew closer, moths to the flame of his vast spirit. Bruce himself disregarded his daughter's own rules about the pours and kept the wine freely flowing out of a bottle in his hand. Ainsley's cup had never been less than half full. She'd estimated that she'd knocked back at least four glasses of the estate Syrah, with its delicious undertones of smoky cigar.

Now the sun had begun its lonely descent towards the tops of the rounded hills to the west. Ainsley slid behind the wheel of her car and started it up and drove towards those hills, holding a hand up to shield her eyeballs from the light of the sunset.

Soon she arrived in downtown Paso Robles, driving down Spring Street. Businesses flashed past—luxurious inns, wine tasting rooms decorated with rustic barrels, high-end donut shops, charming cafes, and Italian restaurants.

Ainsley's mouth was set hard against it all. Her eyes

welled with tears. The betrayal sloshed angrily inside her stomach as loudly as the wine.

She had no place to go, nothing to investigate, no job to worry about. It was a terrible feeling.

Emptiness, loneliness, purposelessness.

She left the city proper and slipped onto an industrial backroad. There were oil change shops, sand & gravel companies, cleaning services, storage unit sites, stores for truck accessories.

Then, at the end of a strip mall, shone a single rectangular white sign. It was small and decently lit.

Renata's Taqueria.

Ainsley brought the car to a halt, smack in the middle of the road. She stared at the restaurant.

"Okay," she said, "one more shot."

She turned the wheel and pulled into the parking lot.

CHAPTER TWENTY-TWO

Ainsley was seated at the humble four-top in the taqueria, which at five pm was empty except for one old man in a booth. He was wearing a green baseball cap and mechanically lifted one spoonful of soup after another to his mouth.

A middle-aged woman brought her a bowl of chips with red salsa. The woman was wearing black stretch pants and white Reeboks and her lustrous black hair was pushed up on the back of her head with a green clip.

Ainsley smiled at her. She left a menu and went away behind the counter. A phone was crooked into her ear and she was alternately listening in silence, then talking in rapid Spanish. Ainsley couldn't make it out.

At last the woman hung up and came over. "Hello how are you," she said. Her voice carried the light but distinct accent of a second-generation Mexican immigrant.

"I'm good," said Ainsley. "Are you Renata?"

"Yes," she said. "What would you like?"

Ainsley glanced at the menu. "The taco plate."

"What kind you like," came the reply.

"Chicken."

"*Tres tacos de pollo*," Renata said, writing it dutifully on her small pad. "Anything to drink?"

"You have horchata?"

"Sorry, we are out."

"You have any cousins instead?"

Renata's pencil stopped moving. "Excuse me?"

Ainsley kept her frame strong; she was committed now. The wine was doing its part to embolden her as well.

"Instead of the horchata, I'll take one cousin named Fernando," she said.

"It's a joke or something?" the woman said.

Ainsley leaned back and opened her body up, arms and legs wide. She wanted to show she was no threat. "Bruce Falston told me that Fernando didn't show up for work today."

Renata's eyes went wide. She turned and hightailed it into the kitchen. The swinging door swung back and forth behind her, then came to a rest.

Alone at her table, Ainsley sighed. This was going about as poorly as she imagined it would. She drummed her fingers on the table.

Through the circular window in the swinging door, she saw the faces of Renata and the cook peering out at her. They were making no move to prepare anything.

Ainsley rose to her feet. She'd have to address this directly.

She pushed through the swinging door and went into the kitchen. It was hot and crammed with equipment—warm ovens, utility carts, a food processor, a walk-in refrigerator, a large bubbling stock pot on the stove.

"Excuse me, you can't come in here," said Renata, standing upright as Ainsley entered.

Next to her stood the cook, an old woman with low purple pouches hanging beneath sad eyes. She wore a tired white apron and through the pouches the eyes detachedly studied Ainsley.

"I'm missing my engagement ring," said Ainsley. "I think Fernando stole it from Trebuchet winery. Do you know where he is?"

"Who is Fernando?"

"He's your cousin. You recommended him to work for Bruce Falston."

"I don't know this person."

Ainsley stood there, eyes circling the kitchen as she planned her next move. She'd just run into the same brick wall that federal prosecutors ran into when interrogating members of organized crime. *I dunno, I never heard of the guy.* Stalemate was the logical conclusion of playing dumb.

"Then forget it," Ainsley finally said. "I'll just take an iced tea with the tacos."

She went back out to the dining room and dropped into her chair. She scooped a chip into the salsa and pushed it into her mouth. Across the restaurant, the old man lifted another shaking spoonful of soup to his mouth.

Through the door of the kitchen, Ainsley could see the old woman making the tacos. They weren't going to let her rot, not entirely.

A few minutes later, Renata exited the kitchen with a plate of tacos. She walked over to Ainsley and wordlessly threw them down onto the table. Then she turned on her heel and beelined back into the kitchen.

That was how it was going to be.

Ainsley picked up one of the tacos, suddenly hungry. She'd been drinking on an empty stomach and now it demanded retribution. Each taco consisted of two flat corn tortillas, a small nest of shredded chicken, a sprinkling of cotija cheese, and a tiny spoonful of salsa.

That was how they were supposed to look—and to Ainsley's surprise, they tasted terrific. She'd been worried that the cook might sabotage the plate.

Ainsley polished off the tacos and wiped her mouth. The cook's face was watching her through the circular door. She twinkled her fingers towards the woman. The woman didn't react.

Then Ainsley dropped some cash on the table. It was too much for the meal, but she didn't want to interact with Renata any more by asking for change. She saluted the old man, still lifting the spoon of soup towards his mouth. He didn't react.

She left the restaurant.

———

Outside was dusk.

The rich, cool smell of nighttime mountains had begun to fill the air. Ainsley pulled her jacket more tightly across her body and mentally prepared herself to drive back to La Marmota. It wouldn't be fun navigating the twisty dark country roads at night.

As she crossed the parking lot, a gravelly voice behind her shouted, "Hey."

Ainsley turned. It was the cook, standing outside the taqueria's door. The old woman was still wearing her tired white apron. Behind her, standing safely behind the glass, was Renata. She was glaring.

"I can help you," the cook said. She spoke with a heavier accent than Renata had.

Ainsley tried to keep a blank expression. She strode back towards the entrance to the taqueria.

"Tell me," she said.

"I know Fernando," the cook said. "I know he took that ring. I know where he go to."

"How do you know him?"

"He is the *sobrino* of my ex-husband."

Sobrino meant nephew. Ainsley nodded. "Okay."

"He stay with me for two month. Whole time, I want him to leave."

"Why?"

The woman's eyes flashed angrily. "Because he steal from me too."

"What did he steal?"

"My phone."

"You caught him?" asked Ainsley.

The woman nodded. "Last Saturday I tell him he leave my house in two weeks. This morning I wake up and he is—" She snapped her fingers and thrust her hands out. "*Se fue.*"

That meant *gone*. "So he left early?"

"Yes. He didn't tell me nothing."

"So where did he go?"

The woman's sad purple eye-pouches grew even sadder. "Chicago."

"Why did he go there?"

"My cousin Mateo said he will give better work."

"Where does Mateo work?"

"I don't know. Bars."

"Can I talk to Mateo?"

"I give you his number. Maybe he respond."

The woman pulled her phone out of her pocket and opened her contacts. Ainsley quickly pulled out her own and took a photo of the contact screen. The name read *Mateo Casillas*.

"Thank you very much," said Ainsley.

"I tell him you call. He doesn't like Fernando but he wants to help him."

So Fernando was the family screwup, and they were playing pass-the-trash with him.

"That would be great," said Ainsley. "*Muy amable*."

In the doorway, protected by the glass, Renata scowled. As the chef walked back inside, she smacked the old woman with a towel.

————

Ainsley hadn't driven a minute down the street when her phone rang. It was her brother-in-law.

She put it on speakerphone. "Hey Wayne," she said.

He sounded out of breath. "Ainsley, long time no talk."

"Are you walking the dogs again?"

"You bet. Did you make it to California?"

"Yeah, I'm here in Paso Robles, right now."

"Did you find him?"

"No. Where is he?"

"Headed east on one-seventy-eight. He's nearing Lake Isabella."

"Where do you think he's going?"

"From the map, my guess is he's headed to Death Valley."

Ainsley swore under her breath. "Well, I gotta follow him. I can't quit now. Will you be around for updates?"

"For a few hours, yes."

"Message me."

They disconnected. Ainsley Walker wheeled the car around, made a quick U-turn, and took off towards the desert.

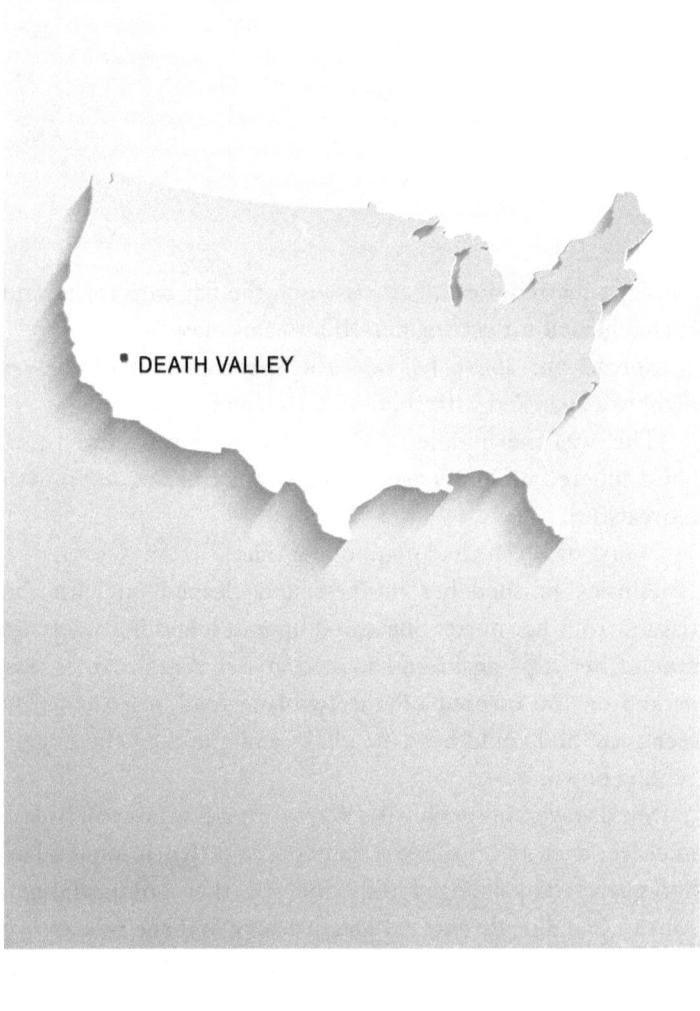

CHAPTER TWENTY-THREE

Ainsley squatted down, bare-assed on the flat bare rocks, and cursed herself for getting herself into this mess.

Spread out above her was the spectacular black desert night sky, spangled with thousands of white points of light.

This was the middle of Death Valley. It was eleven pm. She'd sobered up hours ago. And she was freezing, even with a sweatshirt.

Worst of all, she had no phone service.

Ainsley finished her business and cleaned up with the tissues from her purse. She stood up and hiked her pants up around her hips again and looked at her rental car. It was parked on the turnout off the two-lane road, less than fifty feet away. She could hear the clicks and clinks of the engine cooling down.

She'd stayed in touch with Wayne for a few hours. His last message, over an hour and a half ago, said that it looked like her quarry had changed direction. By that point, though, Ainsley had already entered Death Valley, and she was unsure about what to do, where to go. Without further direction, she'd squinted her eyes and stayed on course, bearing down the narrow strip of black road in front of her hood.

But Wayne hadn't ever followed up. When she'd checked her messages again, she found nothing. Zero bars. No connectivity whatsoever.

It'd freaked her out. The phone was her one remaining connection with sanity. It was her lifeline to the only person on her side, the only one who understood what she was doing, and why it was important.

So she'd kept driving. A sign emerging out of the darkness soon after had informed motorists that there was no cell service until Stovepipe Wells. That was still at least forty minutes away.

Then nature called.

Ainsley balled up the damp tissues and jammed them into her back pocket. She closed her eyes and forced herself to take a deep inhale. Then she forced a long exhale. Then another, and another.

When she opened her eyes, she felt calmer. She would drive to Stovepipe Wells and find a network there.

———

Nearly an hour later, a tall motion-activated sodium light blinked on as Ainsley parked in the lot at the visitor center.

She checked her phone. No networks available.

Seething, she stepped out and walked up to the doors of the center, looking down at her phone. Maybe drawing closer to the center would help. She scanned the available networks again.

Nothing.

She sighed. Down the road, she saw orange lights in the night sky. It was a hotel.

Ainsley ran back to her car and drove over. A sign read *Inn at Furnace Creek*. Judging from the landscaping, the palms, and the exquisite lighting, this was a luxury property.

She pulled into a guest parking spot and popped out of the car again. She ran up the stairs into the lobby.

A sallow man at reception looked up from behind the desk. His name badge read *Ronald M*. "Can I help you?"

"I need to find a mobile network."

He winced and shook his head sadly. "Sometimes you can get one bar with Verizon, but not this time of year."

"How about hotel wifi?"

Ronald paused. "Are you a guest?"

"No."

"Do you have a reservation?"

Ainsley shook her head.

"Sorry." He shrugged. "Is there something you need me to look up..."

He let the sentence die. Ainsley changed tack. "I tried the visitor center down the street but nothing."

"Jasper shuts off the wifi at night. Mara'll be in at six o'clock if you can wait until then."

"So what am I supposed to do?" said Ainsley. "I don't know where I'm going or what I'm doing."

She regretted her tone immediately. She hadn't meant to sound whiny and desperate.

"I can't help you with that," the man said. "Also you can't stay here."

Ainsley looked out a window on the other side of the resort. A gorgeous cerulean blue swimming pool was lit up perfectly—and beyond, nothing but flat rock stretching out into the inky night. She wondered how much water evaporated out of the pool every day in this climate.

The front desk clerk guessed her intentions. "Miss, please

don't sleep in the desert either. There's night snakes and spotted skunks. Mountain lions too."

"Okay."

"If you come back at five when our café opens, I can sell you some coffee and a pastry."

Ainsley nodded, humbled. "That's very nice of you."

Her head hanging low, she left the hotel and slipped into her rental car. She put the car into drive and drove off.

————

At four in the morning, laying in the cold backseat of her rental car, Ainsley came to a big realization.

Beds weren't overrated.

Not in the least. They are exactly as great as they seem.

It'd been a dark night of the soul. She'd pulled off the road into a low gully and parked the car and climbed into the backseat. She prayed it wouldn't rain, since Death Valley was known for its flash floods in gullies just like this.

And then she began to turn over scenarios in her mind. According to Wayne, the Legal Weasel had changed direction, which meant that he'd changed his mind about something. God only knew how many frenzied little confused thoughts were flying through his cranium like bats. Maybe he'd turned around and gone back to Bakersfield. He could've headed south into Los Angeles. He could've pointed his car north towards Fresno. The woman he was with could be manipulating him, controlling him to do her bidding.

For some reason, the thought of that made Ainsley's blood boil. That woman had no right.

Then she stopped herself. What was she *doing*? These feelings of ownership were silly and needed to go. She had to smash them, sweep the shards into a dustpan, and toss them into a dumpster.

Instead, Ainsley fixated on knowns, on facts. She knew two things for sure. One was that this man she'd married had carried a lot of secrets. The other was that she needed to track him down to find out what happened to her ring. The Mexicans in Paso Robles, and the connection to Chicago, was a tempting distraction. But she wouldn't let that deter her. She still needed to hear the story direct from him.

The eastern half of the horizon began to glow a deep purple.

———

At six am, Ainsley sat in the café of the resort, eyes bleary. Her finger compulsively reloaded the network setting on her phone, which lay flat on the small table next to her untouched jelly donut and black coffee.

"Come on," she said.

The desert was illuminated orange now. On the other side of the bright blue swimming pool, the flat dun-colored rock stretched for miles, up to the foot of the Panamint Mountains that towered over the valley. She hadn't been able to see the range last night, in the dark.

She flicked her finger again—and there it was. The visitor center network was now enabled. She quickly connected.

Two voice notes popped up. Both were from Wayne.

From last night: "*Hey, you stopped responding so I guess you're out of service. I got him on the road to Vegas. It's basically for sure. Nobody goes to Barstow for fun. I'll verify in the morning.*"

And then, from not more than fifteen minutes earlier: "*Hey Ainsley, so I was right. He's at a hotel in Vegas. Message me for more.*"

Ainsley rocketed to her feet. "Hey Ronald?"

The night reception guy was crossing the lobby, yawning,

carrying a small stack of paper in his hands, presumably the night audit report.

"Yes?" he said.

"How far is Las Vegas from here?"

"Two and a half hours."

Ainsley saluted him. She would be there by eight.

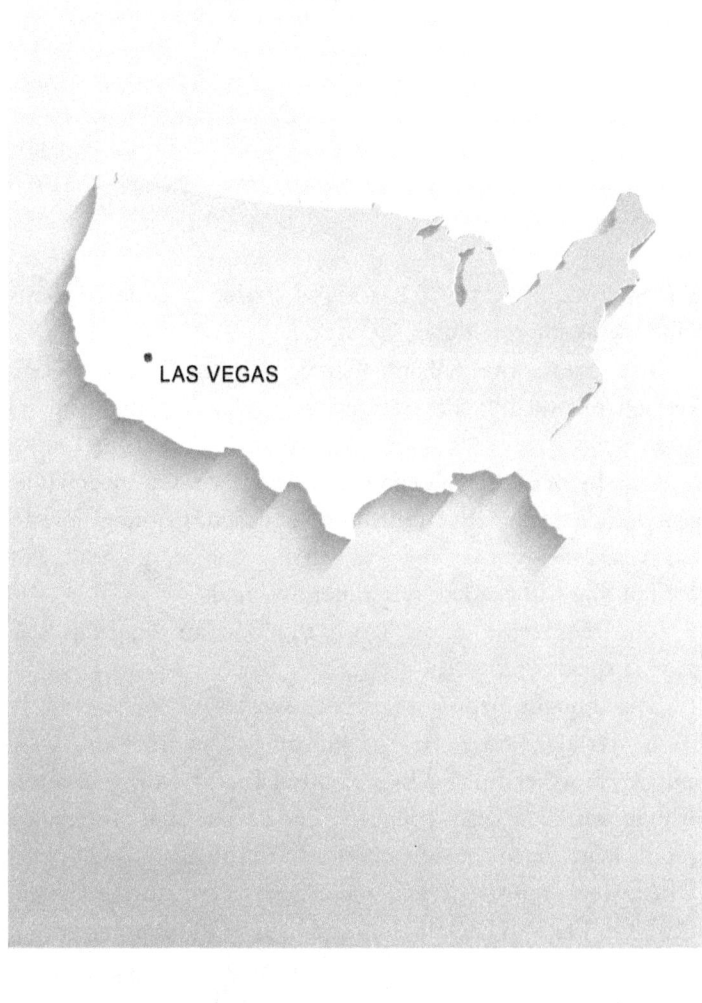

CHAPTER TWENTY-FOUR

The sun-caked hotels of Las Vegas sizzled outside Ainsley's windows as she tore down the Strip.

The Strat, the Sahara, Circus Circus. The Venetian loomed tall on her left, its vertical stripes climbing up its three wings.

One by one, they all came and went. Ainsley, meanwhile, was preoccupied with thoughts of Chicago. Coming here to Las Vegas meant that she was missing out on her lead. But she felt like still needed to find her husband.

The realization came like a thunderclap. She was still playing the dutiful wife.

The thought made her nearly choke.

It was eight-fifteen in the morning. The sidewalks were mostly empty, except for loose-panted chefs heading either to or from work. In Vegas you never knew what kind of schedule people kept, since time meant almost nothing.

Ainsley's nose twitched in disgust. She'd always felt an allergy to Las Vegas. Gambling and drugs and stripping struck her as stupid and tawdry. She'd been invited on a girls' trip to Vegas once, years ago, and she'd started checking her watch on the morning of the second day. It'd been a long, expensive weekend filled with annoyance and boredom.

As she waited to turn left, her screen lit up with a new message: *He just arrived at the airport. Terminal 3.*

Dammit. Biting her lip, Ainsley put on her turn signal and swung back into the main lanes, ignoring the horns of the cars she'd just cut off. She pointed the nose of her rental car toward the Harry Reid International Airport, which lay just south of town.

"Jared," she said aloud, "you stupid bastard, stay put for one goddamn hour."

———

At the airport, she flew into the visitors' parking, turned off the engine, and leapt out of the car. She walked briskly into Terminal 3 and texted Wayne along the way.

Where?

The east end. I can't see any more than that.

Ainsley ran into the check-in level and turned left. She walked quickly through the crowds of travelers, some flush with winnings, others staggering sloppy drunk straight off the nightclub floor, and still others dressed for business.

Her eyes roved the faces, looking for the Legal Weasel. A thousand thoughts pinged through her mind and she was curious which one would win the race to fly out of her mouth first, whenever she finally saw him.

She passed check-in counters for Copa, Aeromexico, Korean Air. They were all international airlines.

He's leaving the country.

Her insides tightened, her pace quickened.

A zigzagged line of nearly a hundred people waited ahead. That was the security line. Ainsley scanned the faces as she approached.

Then her heart dropped to her knees.

It was him.

————

Her legal spouse, Jared Walker.

She would know his face anywhere. The insouciant quar-ter-smile. The good-boy short haircut that dipped ever-so-slightly inward at the temples. The fine lines at the corners of his eyes. The way his chin always tipped up for no good reason.

And the inscrutable eyes.

He stood at the front of the security line. He was holding his passport and his tickets.

Next to him was a woman. She was probably a beautiful woman if you had a doll fetish. She looked nothing like Ains-ley: prim, plastic, personality-less. She wore a figure-hugging one-piece purple cocktail dress—at eight o'clock in the morning—and her huge shock of black hair fell in lustrous waves down her back. She had other blessings that were more noticeable and had likely cost quite a bit.

Before Ainsley could decide how to approach, they'd stepped forward to the TSA authority at the podium. The officer checked their tickets, scanned their passports, and waved them through. It'd taken twenty seconds, and they were gone.

Ainsley stood on her tiptoes. The Legal Weasel had laid his carry-on bag on the stainless-steel counter and he was taking off his shoes and pulling off his belt.

It was too late. Ainsley couldn't cause a scene and risk disrupting the airport. She'd have federal security all over her, be detained, maybe arrested. It would impact everything in her life.

Dammit.

Her fingers clenched into a pair of fists. She saw him step into the full-body scanner and lift his arms over his head. Then she saw his female companion fix her hair before doing the same.

A rage began to fill Ainsley's body. She stamped it down.

And then, a moment later, on the other side of the scanner, the Legal Weasel and the woman collected their bags from the conveyor—and disappeared out of sight.

He was gone. Really and truly—not just out of sight, but out of their marriage.

Ainsley's feelings were a crowded pen of cats, all fighting for dominance. Fury, relief, happiness, disappointment, irrational joy. She was struggling through all of them, all at once.

Ainsley went over and dropped onto an open bench. Next her sat to a boy wearing a pair of huge headphones. He was playing a game on a Switch. Ainsley put a hand over her mouth, trying to fight back her feelings. Onscreen the boy's avatar was swimming through a large aquarium, smashing fish with a hammer. The boy was too busy to notice her.

Ainsley might as well have been invisible.

She sensed that she was about to lose the battle with the crowded feelings. She put her face into her hands and felt the tears begin. Soon her cheeks had grown wet. Her shoulders convulsed.

Nobody noticed.

A man came over and tapped the boy on the shoulder. The boy stood up and followed his father, leaving Ainsley on the bench.

Alone.

———

Half an hour later, Ainsley remained on the same bench, a pile of damp crumpled tissues next to her. She could feel the heat from the airport glass wall behind her. In the desert, the sun was a stalker.

Unlike the sun, Ainsley was ready to give up.

At the moment, she wasn't very functional. The full weight of her personal crisis was finally striking her, and she needed to process it.

She'd cycled through all the feelings, trying them out, each one taking its turn in the spotlight like a line of models on a catwalk. She didn't have any favorites. None of them were clear winners.

Something was abundantly clear, though. For weeks, one part of Ainsley had needed to talk to her husband and find out why he'd walked out. But an equal part of her, maybe even bigger, hadn't cared enough to ask. That part had given up on him—for how long, she wasn't sure—and had really only cared about finding her engagement ring.

Discovering that the other part of her existed was devastating. She'd always valued relationships, and she'd never understood how people could be so callous towards their intimate partners. It was terrifying to know that a small version of that callous person had been crouched inside of her.

She'd been toggling between the two for long enough.

That part of her was also the part that adored gemstones. Minerals and objects couldn't hurt you, she rationalized. They couldn't lie to you, damage you, abandon you for no reason. You could place your trust in them.

Her phone rang. The screen read Wayne.

Ainsley blew her nose and arranged her hair. It was pointless for a phone call but that didn't matter.

"Hi Wayne," she said, putting the phone underneath her hair to her ear.

"Did you find him?"

"Yeah," she said, "but he was already going through security."

"That sucks. I was rooting for you."

"Thanks."

"He's still in the airport. You could buy a ticket somewhere."

"Yeah," said Ainsley, a note of tired sadness in her voice.

"What's the matter?"

Then she closed her eyes and heard the new words fall out of her mouth like baby birds tumbling out of their nest.

"I don't think I'm going to follow him anymore."

"Really?"

"Yeah."

"Why not?"

"He left my ring at a winery. Now it's been stolen by a Mexican guy who's on his way to Chicago."

"I thought you wanted to talk to him though? Find out what's been happening?"

She turned her head and stared deeply at some undesignated point outside the window.

"No, I don't," she finally said.

"He walked out on your marriage, for no reason."

"I know."

"He didn't give an explanation."

"I know."

"He didn't even give *me* an explanation."

"Look," she said, "my ring is going in one direction, and my husband is going in another. I have to choose between them. So this is my decision."

He paused. She heard the sound of his breathing. "Okay," he finally replied. "It's your decision."

"I could be good at it, don't you think?" said Ainsley.

"At what?"

"Tracking missing gemstones."

"You've always been very persistent."

"And I know a lot about them."

"You do."

It was true. She'd been studying them for most of her adult life. She'd even completed a survey course at GIA, the Gemological Institute of America, and had the certificate to prove it, back when she thought her career might be headed towards jewelry. It hadn't, but there could be time to change that.

"Even better," added Wayne, "what if you could get people to send you to foreign countries to find missing gemstones?"

International mysteries. That was the dream, wasn't it? Something to unite her love of gemstones with her other great love—travel.

"A girl can wish," she said. "Anyways, thanks for your help, Wayne."

"All right," he replied, "and I'll be in touch if I hear anything else. Just know you've got a friend over here."

"That means a lot to me," she said.

"Keep in touch, Ainsley."

She ended the call. Then she stood up and stood at the window and watched the travelers rushing into the airport. She felt the sun's heat on her face and shoulders. She was bathed in light.

"A gemstone detective," she said.

CHAPTER TWENTY-FIVE

The iconic Chicago skyline hovered in the distance, five miles south, as Ainsley walked north along the lakeside path.

Her destination: Uptown, a historic neighborhood on the north side of the city. Ainsley knew it from her previous visits. It'd been the epicenter of Chicago nightlife a century earlier, with iconic bars like The Green Mill and the massive Uptown Theater, which used to seat over five thousand people but had been sealed shut for decades. Al Capone had ruled this neighborhood, and his army of bootleggers had rolled barrels of liquor from the smugglers' boats on the lakefront up Lawrence Avenue into a network of underground storage tunnels. He'd once blown up the local home of a district attorney who'd dared to challenge him.

The neighborhood had fallen on hard times in the nineteen-fifties. Poor immigrants arriving in Chicago found cheap beds and cheap hotels there. Desperately broke Vietnamese immigrants had set up their own small community. The state had used it as a dumping ground for mentally ill people. Every other block had a shelter for battered women. For decades,

Uptown carried a reputation for low rents and low expectations.

But things had changed.

Ainsley turned off from the lake and walked inland. First she noticed the young blonde woman in yoga pants pushing a baby stroller. That was a new sight here. Then she saw the artisanal coffee shops, with their artfully distressed wooden countertops and scores of young men hunched over MacBooks. On the sidewalks, gay couples passed by, openly holding hands while walking their French bulldogs. Plus there were teardowns happening on every block, the decrepit bungalows replaced by gleaming new three-story apartments.

There was a word for this.

Gentrification.

Ainsley redirected her thoughts. Her purpose was simple: She was here to find Mateo Casillas.

She'd cold called his number that the female cook had given her. A voicemail recording announced that Partido Food and Beverage was unavailable, please leave a message. Ainsley'd hung up, then quickly run an online search. Partido Food and Beverage was a vendor, owned by Mateo B. Casillas, age 57, of Chicago. It was contracted with several nightlife venues, including Thalia Hall in Pilsen, Lincoln Hall in Lincoln Park, and the Aragon Ballroom in Uptown.

Here, in this neighborhood.

And there was a concert at the Aragon tonight. She'd studied Mateo's face on his LinkedIn profile and took a screenshot, just to be sure. He was clean shaven with a purple birthmark splashed on his left cheek.

Ainsley found her way down Lawrence Avenue. It was only five pm, but the first concertgoers had begun to queue up alongside the outer wall of the theater, just below the Red Line of the El.

She looked at the marquee. It was a formerly popular grunge rock band called Catbird. They'd had several hits in the nineties but nothing new since the turn of the century. They played primarily to a cadre of older white fans who'd stuck with them through the years as a memory of their adolescence.

Ainsley found the small box office window. "Is there a ticket available for tonight?"

"Yes."

"How much?"

"Fifty plus fees."

"What row?"

"You've never been here?"

"No," said Ainsley, "why?"

"There's no seats, honey."

Ainsley shelled out the money, slipped the ticket into her bag, and walked up the street to wait at a brewpub.

At eight pm she joined the back of the entrance line, which had grown to nearly a thousand. Several of the fans wore small yellow birds perched on their shoulders; others sported orange cat ears on their heads.

At eight thirty pm, the doors opened.

———

Ainsley moved down the elongated entry hall of the Aragon Ballroom. Its low ceiling put psychological pressure on the concertgoers to move forward. She kept an eye out for free-standing bars. One, on the left, wasn't open. Another, on the right, was staffed by a young woman.

No Mateo yet.

The stream of concertgoers reached the wide double staircase, and she followed it up around the curve. It emptied out into a vast open parquet floor, large enough to hold a few thousand people. The stage awaited at one end, while overhead twinkled a bright blue ceiling lit with a thousand stars.

Ainsley sucked in her breath. It was beautiful.

This room had a long history. They'd held swing dancing competitions here in the nineteen-forties. In the nineteen-fifties, nationally syndicated radio programs had broadcast big band music from its dance floor. In fact, nearly every major musical act of the last eighty years had played here on their way to the top. At other times, the space had been used as a site for fundraisers, including President Obama's fiftieth birthday party.

Ainsley scanned the theater for bars. There were four, two on either side of the theater, beneath a dark Moorish-style arcade that ringed the room. All four were open, all four had lines of people.

She walked past the first two. Both were staffed by older women. Then she crossed to the other side of the theater.

There.

It was Mateo: she was sure of it. He was a short man, moving at lightning speed behind the bar, accepting cash and shoving plastic cups of beers and cocktails. Ainsley was getting tired just watching him. In the darkness, a purple splash of a birthmark was a blur on his left cheek.

The line for drinks was getting longer. This would be the worst time to approach him. She would wait.

Ainsley leaned against a pillar and crossed her arms.

———

The lights went down, and a roar went up from the crowd. The opening act took the stage, a guitar-bass-drums trio composed of three balding men who'd had a minor hit when

Ainsley was in junior high. The singer tried to crack a joke that the average weight of the audience was exceeded only by their average age. It went poorly. The band left the stage after only five songs.

Ainsley peered over at the bar. Mateo was still shoveling drinks and grabbing cash like there was no tomorrow.

She felt eyes upon her. A pair of paunchy middle-aged men wearing black-and-yellow Catbird shirts were eyeballing her. She sensed they'd been watching her for a while.

One twinkled his fingers at her. She looked away. When she looked back, he was already approaching her. His oily black hair needed a wash, and he had an extrovert's big grin. A sleeve of tattoos ran down his right arm. Ainsley didn't get any kind of specific vibes from him. He might be the kind of guy you shouldn't trust with a toddler, but on the other hand he might very well turn out to be a world-class dad.

She wondered if people wondered the same thing about her.

"I told him not to make that joke," the guy said, opening.

"The singer?" replied Ainsley.

"Yeah." Then he added casually, "I'm friends with the band."

"It was a bad choice."

"Naw, they're family guys now. Their party days ended a long time ago."

"I mean the joke was the bad choice," she said.

He ignored her. "Why are you here alone, tied to a pillar?"

"It's a long story."

"Do you have a boyfriend?"

"I have a husband," she said.

His eyes glanced to her finger. "You don't have a ring."

"That's why I'm here. I'm trying to find it."

"How?"

"It's complicated."

He drew closer. "I'm all ears. My name's Brian."

Ainsley chewed over her options. If she told him her story, he might be able to help her. That was the best-case scenario. The worst-case scenario was that she would have to disappear into the crowd and avoid him for the rest of the night. That wasn't too bad an option, all things considered.

"I'm Ainsley," she said, shaking hands. "I'm looking for a young guy named Fernando. He works over there." She gestured towards the bar.

"He's one of Mateo's guys?"

Ainsley bolted to full attention. This guy knew Mateo by name. That was worth something.

"Yeah," she said.

"Mateo has a lot of employees," said the guy. "They're not all accounted for, if you know what I'm saying."

She nodded. Ainsley had figured that Fernando's immigration status was questionable anyways. There were thirteen million people like him in the United States, living in the shadows, cleaning people's houses, cooking people's food, cutting people's hair, pruning people's vines. They existed in a legal gray area that had emerged only because of the American economy's need for cheap labor. The federal legislative branch had been deadlocked for decades over how to resolve the issue.

"Can I buy you a beer?" he said.

"No thanks," she replied.

"Can you buy me one?"

She laughed despite herself. "That's pretty good."

"I was serious."

"Okay."

Just then, the lights went down again, and Catbird took the stage. "Come stand with me and my friend," Brian said.

"Why?"

"We'll entertain you with smart jokes," he replied, "and we'll keep the dumb guys away."

He winked. Ainsley smiled. He was talking her language now. She reluctantly peeled herself off the pillar.

CHAPTER TWENTY-SIX

Music had changed a lot since the nineties, but Catbird hadn't gotten the news.

Their concert started with a sonic blast of midrange guitars. The group had three guitarists in total—all playing the same four-chord progression, all playing the same continuous quarter-note downstrokes. Behind them, the bass guitarist and the drummer kept a dirge-like tempo, their heads down.

To Ainsley, it sounded like audio sludge.

She hadn't been a fan of grunge rock. She'd been born a bit too late to enjoy it properly. Plus, the little she'd heard—Nirvana, Pearl Jam, Alice in Chains, Soundgarden—hadn't made her want to dance, or really do much of anything except mope. It didn't help that their lead singers kept committing suicide.

The Catbird singer, a slight guy in wraparound shades, seized the microphone and began keening and caterwauling lyrics that were impossible to decipher. He wore a black t-shirt and black pants and black boots. So did the five other guys in the band. These days, that was the mandatory outfit for dad rock.

"Don't they sound good?" shouted her new friend into her ear.

"Oh yeah, definitely!" she shouted back.

The fourth song started with a promising drum fill, and soon it sounded just like the first three. Ainsley grew bored, shifting her weight from one foot to another. She looked over at the bar. The line for Mateo was as short as she'd seen it.

She felt a tug at her elbow. Brian had noticed her looking over there. "I'll introduce you to Mateo later," he said.

"How do you know him?" she said back.

"All the staff knows me, I come to almost every show here," he said.

That sounded evasive. "I have to go to the bathroom," she said.

"It's downstairs," Brian said.

His eyes followed Ainsley as she went to the rear of the ballroom and down the stairs.

———

After stepping out of the ladies' restroom, she climbed the stairs and entered the vast main room. At Mateo's bar, only four people waited in line.

She joined them. Catbird thundered onstage; the crowd threw its arms forward. Ainsley was happy that crowd liked the music, even if she didn't care much for it.

At last she stepped forward to face Mateo. He was wiping down the bottles and the countertop as quickly as possible. "What do you want?"

"I need Fernando to make my drink," she said.

"Why?"

"He made me a good drink last time."

"Tonight is his first night back this year."

"It was a while ago."

Mateo grew irritated. "He's on break and I can make everything better than him. What do you want?"

"A rum and coke."

Mateo's hands flew across the station. First the plastic cup, then a scoop of ice, next a drizzle of clear liquid from the upside-down bottle of Bacardi, and finally the soft drink nozzle filling the cup to the brim.

"Eleven-fifty," he said.

Behind Mateo, a young guy arrived wheeling a dolly. He was skinny, with an ugly puppet face, wearing a black Partido Food & Beverage t-shirt.

"Fernando!" said Ainsley.

The kid looked up, startled.

Bingo. It was a guess, but he'd responded. Mateo rolled his eyes. "Eleven-fifty," he repeated.

Ainsley pushed some money at him, took her drink, accepted the change, and moved a short distance away. She watched the helper.

Fernando was working as the bar back. He was stacking bottles, tossing empties into a sack, wiping down the counter, replacing the lime wedges. He discreetly checked his phone when he thought Mateo wasn't looking, until Mateo threw an empty cup at him.

He was also wearing flat-soled soccer shoes. It didn't seem unintentional or accidental. They were a choice.

Catbird played its final song of the main set, and during the enormous noise from the crowd that followed, a wave of people engulfed the bar. Fernando began making drinks as fast as his hands allowed, which was still slower than Mateo. Ainsley watched Mateo shout "venga" at him. *Let's go!*

She felt a hand across her shoulders. It was her new friend Brian. "They're going to be slammed from now on," he said, "and security is going to sweep us out after the show ends. You want to wait for them outside, after the show?"

"I already found Fernando," said Ainsley.

"You explained your situation with the ring?"

She hung her head. "No, not yet."

"We'll find them after the show, outside. Mateo knows me."

He tilted his head in an indication to join him back on the main floor.

Ainsley allowed herself to be led back into the center of the floor as Catbird returned for an encore.

———

An hour later, Ainsley was standing on the sidewalk alongside the long east wall of the theater, shivering in the cold. The employee access door was along the back. Her ears were buzzing from the volume of the PA stacks.

Nearby, under the overpass, a line of temporary food stands had been set up, with Latino cooks dishing out hot taco plates as fast as they could. Hungry white concertgoers stuffed the steaming food into their mouths with cold fingers, and wiped their lips with paper napkins.

Brian and his friend wore hoodies and shorts, but their legs seemed unbothered by the cold. They stood there, exchanging stories of the best shows they'd seen around town. Two aging scenesters, Midwest style, chatting about Wilco, Disturbed, Urge Overkill, other alt-rock bands that had been mostly forgotten.

"Do you like Fall Out Boy?" said Brian.

"I don't really remember their music," she replied.

"Good answer," said the friend.

"We were gonna have to dump you if you said yes," added Brian.

"Are they from Chicago?" asked Ainsley.

"Yeah, but we don't like to admit that," replied the friend.

Brian swung his hands together. "So what happened with this guy Fernando?"

Ainsley took a deep breath. "My husband left me last month and disappeared with my engagement ring. But then someone stole my engagement ring from him, and I'm ninety percent sure it was this kid Fernando."

"So you're trying to get the ring back?"

"Yes."

"But not the husband."

She shook her head no. "He left me without a word. Screw him."

Brian crooked his eyebrow. "No explanation?"

"None."

"Why not just let it go?"

"That ring is the only thing I can control in this whole stupid situation. It's hard to explain. I just need it back."

A small noise nearby drew their attention. It was Mateo, exiting the theater and heading towards the tiny employee parking lot next door. Behind him trailed Fernando, wearing a heavy red parka.

"Mateo!" shouted Brian, raising his hand.

The food-and-beverage contractor turned. "What's happening, guys?"

The two locals strolled over, Ainsley following discreetly behind.

Brian said, "Doing good bro! Do you still have the contract at the Thalia Hall? We didn't see you on Friday."

"No, we lost it," said Mateo.

"For now."

"It's competitive," Mateo said. His eyes flicked over to Ainsley. A glimmer of recognition passed over his face.

Fernando stood on the passenger side of a blue sedan, his

hand on the door. Ainsley tried to make eye contact, but the kid looked away.

"Did you meet Ainsley already?" said Brian.

She stepped forward and presented her hand. Mateo looked at her, slightly confused, then shook it.

"Inside we met briefly," she said, "but I was really trying to meet Fernando."

Mateo's eyes narrowed. "Why?"

She noticed that he had shifted positioned his body to block her view of the young barback.

"Because I think he has something that belongs to me."

"It's a wedding ring," added Brian.

Mateo turned. Fernando was looking guilty, one hand stuffed deep in his pocket. The boss barked something at him in rapid Spanish—Ainsley couldn't make it out. Fernando shook his head.

"He doesn't have nothing of yours," said Mateo.

"I think he does," she shot back.

"You leave him alone," the Mexican guy warned her. "Don't talk to him."

"What if I do?"

Mateo looked at her with a mixture of sadness and intimidation. "You don't want to find out."

He held up a single index finger and wagged it at her. His eyes were deadly serious. "You don't want no part of this."

"I want my ring. I'll do whatever it takes."

Mateo glanced at Brian and his friend, who'd stepped back. They looked embarrassed by how things had escalated. Then he went to his sedan and unlocked it and both men slipped inside. The doors closed with a thunk. The engine revved, the brake lights lit up cherry red.

"I guess that answers your question," said the friend.

"Yes it does," said Ainsley. "It's clear he was lying."

Brian said, "No, he said that—"

Ainsley shook her head. "He was lying, Brian. Maybe because Fernando was lying. They have my ring. I know it."

The sedan shifted into reverse, and the dual white lights lit up the small parking lot and the back wall of the theater. Ainsley noticed something on the sedan's bumper. A sticker.

"Step aside so they don't run over you," said Brian.

"One second," she said.

She quickly snapped a photo of the bumper sticker on the rear of Mateo's car. Then she moved aside.

The sedan pulled backwards out of the spot and shifted into drive. Ainsley locked eyes with Fernando in the passenger seat for a brief instant—and then the vehicle peeled out of the parking lot.

The three of them watched it turn and disappear down Lawrence Avenue.

Brian's friend assumed a sarcastic tone. "Well, I'd say that went well."

Ainsley opened the photo on her phone and zoomed in on the bumper sticker.

It was an image of a soccer ball with a rectangular goal in the background. Next to it were the words *Alianza Futsal*.

"You guys know what this is?"

"Yeah, that's futsal," said Brian. "There's a futsal facility over on Clark near Andersonville. Not too far from here."

"What's futsal?" said Ainsley.

"It's like indoor soccer," said Brian.

Ainsley remembered Fernando's flat-soled soccer shoes. This was her lead.

"I'm going over there tomorrow," she said.

"Not a good idea."

"I don't care."

Summoning all his courage, Brian squared up on Ainsley. "Look, we're strangers. But I feel like you're going to get hurt without someone to back you up. So I'll go with you, just to make sure you're safe."

Ainsley smiled. "That's very sweet."

"Give me your number," he said, handing her his phone.

As Ainsley accepted the phone and entered her phone number, Brian and his friend exchanged a quiet fist bump.

CHAPTER TWENTY-SEVEN

The next morning, Ainsley followed Brian through the glass double doors of the Chicago Futsal Factory.

On the outside, it was an unassuming building, a cross between a strip mall and an industrial building, but inside was a different story. She was greeted by the sights and sounds of thirty children playing soccer on three different small fields. Their parents stood along the sidelines in heavy parkas.

"Go Breanna—"

"Don't let him turn, Jaden—"

"Taylor, stop *playing* with it—"

Near the entrance was the office, and past that was a large bar and grill, with televisions playing international matches.

"Where do you want to start?" said Brian.

"Let's ask those parents," said Ainsley.

She approached a dad. His hands were intertwined in the nets that were hung from the low ceiling and that delineated the out-of-bounds line. His intense eyes were utterly focused on the game: they tracked every movement on the pitch. Ainsley marked him immediately as the type of overinvolved parent who thought his child's every step on the athletic field was a matter of life and death.

"Excuse me," said Ainsley, "when do the adult Latino teams arrive?"

"The Alianza league?"

"Yeah," she said, "that's it."

He checked his watch. "They should be coming in soon. Their games start at noon."

"Thanks."

Ainsley strolled the area, looking at the fierce competition. The children wore shin guards and jerseys and were playing five-a-side, less than half the size of traditional outdoor matches.

Brian joined her with two paper cups of coffee. He offered one. "So what type of guys do you typically date?"

"I've only been single for a few weeks," she said.

"Before you got married, I mean."

"I don't know. I don't think I had a type."

"I'm just trying to find out if I have a shot here."

At that moment, an eight-year-old girl danced around two defenders and poked the ball into the goal with her toe.

"That kid had a shot, and she took it," said Ainsley.

"And so the children shall guide us," he sighed.

The glass entry doors opened, and a group of young Latino guys entered. They carried water bottles and athletic bags. Taking up a strip of open turf on the side of a field, they peeled off their track pants, revealing shorts. Then they put on flat-soled indoor soccer shoes, and finally donned white-and-green jerseys. Ainsley could read the words *Los Queretanos*.

"They look like they know what they're doing," said Brian.

"I wouldn't bet against them."

Even more teams poured in the door in the next few minutes. At five minutes to noon, the referees all blew their whistles, signaling the end of the games. The changeover began. The children left their fields, hugged by their parents, and made their way to the changing rooms.

The Latino guys lifted the nets and entered the field and began warming up.

"Do you see him?" said Ainsley.

"Not yet," said Brian.

The whistles blew for kickoff. All three fields were now occupied by five-on-five matches.

Compared with full eleven-vs-eleven outdoor games, these matches were small. The men moved with quick little steps and tiny flicks. The ball rarely left the ground. It was strategic sport, dependent less on athleticism and more on footwork.

"This feels like basketball," said Brian.

"A lot," said Ainsley. Then she said, "Look."

Through the glass entry door entered another young Latin guy. He was skinny, wearing a black warmup tracksuit, a black winter cap, and black sunglasses.

He removed the cap and the sunglasses and looked around. She recognized that face instantly.

It was Fernando.

———

Ainsley shrank back and flattened herself against the wall behind them. Without the bright sodium lights that illuminated the playing fields, the edges of the space stayed in darkness. It would be hard for Fernando to see her here.

Brian joined her. They watched the young thief strip off his warmup outfit and stand at the edge of the furthest field, his hands on the net, until a player came off. Then he slipped under the net onto the field and joined the play.

"So what do you want to do?" Brian said.

Her eyes fell on Fernando's pile of clothing. "I want to look through the pockets of his track suit."

"I can grab it."

"Are you sure?"

"Yeah, I'll just drop something next to it. Nobody's gonna bother me either. Not with these mad-dog eyes."

She looked over at him. That was probably true. Brian was the same size and weight as a household refrigerator, the type of guy with a large amount of muscle buried beneath the obvious fat. Anybody who wanted to mess with him needed to bring something extra besides their fists.

"Let's be quick about it," she said.

She watched Brian casually saunter around the fields, hands in the pocket of his hoodie. On the field, Fernando was deep in the gameplay. He didn't notice Brian drop his phone, bend down to pick it up, and quickly scoop up the black track suit.

Brian quietly stuffed it under his hoodie, where it just looked like more excess bodyweight. He sauntered back over to Ainsley.

In the dimness, they quickly rifled through the kid's belongings. There was a phone, which displayed a selfie of his own ugly face, tongue out, on the lock screen. A set of rolling papers and a bag of weed. A butterfly knife.

And a thin wallet.

Ainsley removed the identification. It was a Mexican national ID. The name read Fernando Gaviria. The home address was listed in Sinaloa.

"No ring," Brian said, looking through the pockets of the warmup jacket.

"I wasn't expecting him to be carrying it on his person," she replied. "He might have even sold it. But I'm gonna take a photo of this."

"It's almost halftime, so hurry up."

Ainsley quickly snapped a photo of the identification, then shoved it back in his wallet. Brian stuffed all the clothing under his hoodie again, casually stood up and strolled around the fields. Fernando was still playing, and Brian quietly watched the game for a minute, then discreetly dumped the tracksuit on the ground.

When he got back to Ainsley, he said, "Buy you a beer?"

She didn't answer.

"What's the matter?" he said.

"It's him."

Brian turned. Into the facility had walked Mateo. He walked past the playing fields and into the attached bar and grill.

"Can I buy you a beer?" said Ainsley.

"I thought you'd never ask," Brian replied.

CHAPTER TWENTY-EIGHT

The bar-and-grill was packed with English Premier League supporters. It was match day across the pond in the UK, and the Chicago locals had worn the kits of their favorite teams. Today was Chelsea versus Manchester City.

Brian and Ainsley stood alongside a wall, beers in hand, facing one another. His eyes kept flicking between her face and the action on the television screen over her shoulder. Ainsley didn't have much trouble ignoring the screen over his shoulder.

Her eyes were fixed on Mateo.

The food-and-beverage manager was seated at a folding table with four other people. All five were decked out in the light blue of Manchester City. An icy pail of Corona beers sat on the table between them, and all their chairs were facing one of the screens above the bar.

"You can't just walk up to him," Brian said.

"Why not?" she replied.

"You already blew that last night. He knows you."

"Somebody said she was going to call him for me—"

"Who?"

"His cousin in California, a cook. She was going to put in a good word for me."

Brian finished his beer. "Why don't we focus on Fernando?"

"I will, when his game ends." At that moment, the piercing sound of referees blowing their whistles came from the other room.

"You go find Fernando," said Brian, "and I'll stand right here and watch you. You've got me."

"Okay," said Ainsley, feeling nervous now.

———

Ainsley stood in the middle of the entry doors to the facility. A river of sweat-soaked young Latino guys swarmed past her on their way out of the complex, athletic bags slung over their shoulders. They glowed with post-workout endorphins.

She didn't care about them. She just wanted to get to Fernando. There were no more minutes left for pussyfooting around. It was time.

There he was.

The young thief was walking towards her, chatting with another player, wearing his black track suit jacket. The pants were slung over one arm.

"Fernando Gaviria," she said, stepping directly in his way.

He stopped, startled. "How you know me?"

As he said it, he seemed to recognize her. She gave him a quick reminder. "Last night at the Aragon Ballroom."

"I don't know anything—" he began, protesting.

He tried to get around her, but she blocked his way. "You stole my engagement ring from Trebuchet Winery in Paso Robles, California. Your boss Bruce Falston told me that your aunt worked in the taqueria, and your aunt told me that you had come here to Chicago to work for Mateo." She pushed a finger into Fernando's chest. "Listen to me: I want that ring back. I will pay you for it. I will give you a lot of money."

That was a fib. Ainsley didn't have a lot of money. But she held eye contact with him, showing him that she meant it.

He couldn't look her in the eyes. Ainsley felt a hand pulling her arm. It was the other player, gently pulling her away.

In the blink of an eye, Fernando had burst past her and was out the door.

"Hey!" she shouted.

As Ainsley pivoted, she felt the hand grip her arm even more tightly. She struck the other player in the face with the palm of her free hand. He fell backwards.

"Let me go!"

Ainsley sprinted out the door.

―――――

Outside, she glimpsed Fernando turning left onto Clark Boulevard. In a flash, she was after him. Her prey was about fifty meters ahead on the sidewalk. She accelerated to a sprint, lengthening her stride, pumping her arms.

But Fernando was fast too―just her luck.

He streaked past microbreweries and diners and culinary schools, past the intersection of Foster, and finally into the heart of Andersonville―a longtime lesbian neighborhood that in recent years had seen many heterosexual couples elbow their way into its affordable mortgages and tree-lined residential streets.

The Saturday sidewalks were filled with families, and the young thief dashed through the foot traffic, dodging strollers and slipping around wide groups. A brisk spring chill was in the air, and as Ainsley ran, she felt the tip of her nose growing cold even as her torso grew overheated.

He suddenly cornered down a residential street, and Ainsley followed him, gasping. Fernando was a marvel. An hour of intense soccer, and he still had the cardiorespiratory capacity to outrun her.

He swung the right at the next corner, and when Ainsley got there, she stopped. He'd disappeared. Thirty steps ahead lay another intersection. She ran quickly to that one, then stopped again, looking around in all three directions.

Fernando was nowhere to be seen. Maybe he was cowering in a garbage can. Perhaps he was flattened against the wall of darkened garage. Or possibly he'd simply turned on the afterburners and sprinted so fast that he was out of sight.

"Well, shit," Ainsley said out loud. Then she fell to the grass, gasping for breath.

A pair of women with close haircuts came along the sidewalk. "Hello sweetheart," one said.

Ainsley waved them off, then struggled to her feet and began limping back to the futsal facility.

———

Twenty minutes later, she dragged herself back into the entry doors of the facility. She didn't have to come back, but she wanted to apologize to Brian and tell him what had happened. He'd been so helpful.

In the bar-and-grill, the matches were still playing on the television, but she felt eyes upon her.

Brian was nowhere to be found.

"Excuse me," said a voice.

Ainsley turned. It was a thin Mexican guy wearing a Manchester City jersey. He had scared eyes. "Are you looking for that big guy?"

"Brian?" she said.

"Hoodie and shorts?"

"Yes, that's him."

The guy pointed down the dark hallway that led past the bathrooms. "He went out into the alley."

"Down there?"

"There's a door that goes outside," he said.

"Thanks," she replied.

Ainsley moved out of the crowded sports bar, down the dark hallway. The men's room passed on her left, the women's room on the right. Empty kegs and upside-down stools littered the sides of the hallway. It smelled like stale beer.

At the end of the pitch-black hallway stood a single door. The word EXIT shone above it in red letters. Ainsley placed her hands on the horizontal bar and pushed through.

Sunlight again. She found herself in a Chicago alley.

This was a bit different, however. In front of her, two men stood, watching her. One was nondescript but the other had the face of a rat, twitchy and criminal.

Behind them, a gray SUV stood idling. The back door was open. Inside sat Brian, blindfolded and gagged.

"Get in," said the nondescript one.

"No," she replied.

The rat faced man swung a pistol towards her.

That was persuasive. She dropped her arms to her side. The men approached her.

CHAPTER TWENTY-NINE

Forty minutes later, Ainsley felt the automobile stop.

The men had blindfolded and gagged her. She'd noticed that the rag in her mouth carried the faint taste of gasoline. They'd cuffed her hands—in front, not in back—with a plastic zip tie.

Finally, they'd driven in silence, one of them men sitting between her and Brian. She could feel his tricep pressed against her own. Nobody had said a word the entire ride.

Now, she heard the door open, felt the cool air rush in. Hands pushed her out, then held her up while she found her footing on the ground.

Next, Ainsley was escorted, one hand under each armpit, up a short set of stairs. They were wooden. They felt old and creaked underneath her shoes.

A door squeaked open. She was pushed forward through it. Vinyl flooring under her feet. The ugly scent of moldy linoleum.

From the sound of the echoes of her own footsteps, she knew she was inside a house. An old one. The men led her up another set of stairs. Her shoulder brushed a wooden banister. They were leading her upstairs.

On the second floor, the hands led her into a room and seated her on the edge of a bed. It was an old mattress that sagged under her bottom.

Now she was nervous.

The hands untied the gag and removed it from her mouth. She spat on the floor, ran her tongue around her mouth. Then the hands removed the blindfold from her face.

Ainsley blinked a few times. She was in a decrepit bedroom. Orange shades had been pulled over the windows, suffusing the room with an orange haze. A Mexican guy was studying her from the doorway. He was the same rat-faced one that had pointed the pistol at her. She'd never seen him before.

"Who are you?" she said.

He shook his head no. That would be the best she could get.

"Where am I?"

He ignored that question too. "He'll be here soon."

"Who?"

"You'll see."

The ratfaced man shut the door. She heard the lock click shut, from the outside.

Ainsley looked around. The room was bare. A scuffed, battered dresser leaned against a wall like an exhausted boxer. The mattress sported a thin yellow bedcover but no sheets.

Whatever this was, Ainsley had really gotten mixed up in something.

She sat down again and waited.

———

An hour later, a knock at the door. Ainsley leapt to her feet.

It opened. A small flabby Latin man entered the room, dressed in polo shirt and chinos. He was shaped like a compost heap and his eyes were hard black stones but he carried himself with the no-nonsense air of the president of a company who lived by the creed that time was money.

Behind him stood ratface.

"Ainsley Walker," the boss said.

"How do you know my name?"

He nodded to the ratface, who threw her bag at her. It bounced off her chest and hit the floor.

"That's how."

"Where am I?"

"At a trap house. We use it for sleeping, shelter."

"Who is we?"

Two rows of round white pebbles were revealed in the small man's mouth. It was what passed for a grin. "My name is John."

The way he said it made Ainsley know he was lying.

"Nice to meet you, John. Now let me go."

"They said you're looking for a ring."

"I am."

His eyes narrowed. "Why do you bother my people?"

"The ring is mine. That kid Fernando stole it."

He didn't react, merely studied her. "Why do you think we brought you here?"

"You want the truth?"

"Yes."

"Because I think you guys are involved in something a lot bigger than jewelry or food-and-beverage."

John cocked his head to the side. It was a small admission of truth. "Miss Walker, we don't know why you keep bothering our people. So we have to be cautious."

Suddenly Ainsley understood. They thought she was trying to infiltrate their organization. "Listen, I'm nobody. I'm just an unemployed woman whose husband left her and stole her engagement ring. I was given Mateo's name by—"

He silenced her with a wave of his hand. "It doesn't matter to us what you say, what Mateo say, what Jared say, because we don't know you."

Ainsley's face went hot. *He'd said Jared's name.*

Shit.

In her head, things fell into place. The sudden no-contact disappearance. The unusual visit to Miami. The wine country visit—that was connected too. There was no way that he'd left that ring by accident at Trebuchet winery for Fernando.

It was all connected. But she didn't know how.

"Ainsley, who do you know?"

"Nobody."

"What are you doing here?"

"I want my ring. That's it. I have nothing to give you or tell you."

John's nose twitched in disgust. He left the room without a word. Ratface followed and shut the door. She heard him lock it on the outside.

Their footsteps died away on the staircase. Ainsley heard a door open and close. Then outside a car engine started up. She listened to the sound of the engine pull away.

They'd left her. What she didn't know was if there was anybody else in the house.

She could sit and molder, waiting for her captors to return. Or she could try to break out of the room, and hope the house was empty of anybody else.

Both options were terrible. But only the second one could promise freedom.

She went over to the door and tried the knob. It was firmly locked. With wrists still ziptied together, she went over to her bag, unzipped it, and pulled out her wallet. She removed a department store rewards card. She hadn't used that in years, and they kept her account information on file anyways.

In case the card was suddenly damaged.

She returned to the door and tried to slip the card into the space between the door and the frame. It was a reliable way to pop open a locked door. Ainsley had successfully done it once before, at three in the morning, after locking herself out of her apartment. She hadn't had to call her landlord, which had saved her security deposit.

But this door was tight against the frame, so tight that she couldn't even slip a thin card between the two parts.

Ainsley chewed on her lip as she returned the card to her wallet. She looked for an even thinner card in her bag, but no luck.

She sat down on the bed, cursing silently. Her eyes roved the room, looking for something, anything. It was eerily empty except for the bed, the dresser, heap of old newspapers, and an old cardboard box with empty soda bottles.

Ainsley had an idea.

She walked over to the box and got down on her knees, with some difficulty. She pawed through the empties until she found what she wanted.

A Pepsi bottle with the plastic membrane still wrapped around the bottle, just beneath the screwcap. She lifted the bottle to her teeth and ripped a small bit. Then she peeled the circular scrap of plastic off the bottle.

There.

Ainsley struggled to her feet, then went back to the door. The plastic was significantly thinner than a rewards card, but just as sturdy. She slowly pushed it between the door and the frame.

It slipped in.

Ainsley's eyes went wide. Holding her breath, she carefully brought the plastic down, onto the latching mechanism in the door. She felt it give way.

The door popped open.

CHAPTER THIRTY

For a second, Ainsley froze. She was looking at the short, shabby upstairs hallway. There, just a few feet away, lay the top of the staircase.

No time to think. She picked up her bag and moved as quietly as possible through the hallway and began descending the staircase.

Creak.

It sounded like a gunshot in the quiet house. It had come from the decrepit wooden step under her foot. Ainsley froze again. She was going to be discovered, for sure.

The sound died away. She stood there, arms out hesitantly.

Nothing. The house was silent once again.

She was alone.

Exhaling, Ainsley descended to the dirty main room. Two battered green-and-brown plaid couches had been hurled against opposite walls. A long plastic folding table and several folding chairs lay between them; two new bench platform scales awaited duty. At the far end of the room, a flatscreen television had been balanced on a stack of plastic sheeting.

Ainsley didn't want to think too much about what this house could be used for.

She moved swiftly into the kitchen, which looked like it hadn't been used for decades. She looked down at the floor, then quickly lifted her head up. The linoleum truly was as bad as it had smelled on the way in.

She pushed out the back kitchen door and into the cool sunshine. She descended the steps quickly and circled around the driveway that ran alongside the house. In the front yard, a broken-down green sedan was parked on what remained of the grass.

Ainsley held her bag in her hands, doing her best to conceal the ziptie, and moved swiftly past the sedan and onto the sidewalk.

As she was leaving the property, a sound behind her caught her ear.

It was a knocking. The way a human might knock, to gain attention.

She stopped. Turned.

In the dormer window of the second floor was the shape of a man's head.

Ainsley recognized the shape of that head. It was Brian.

She stood there, stock still, watching him wave his ziptied hands at her. She lifted her own towards him, managing a smile.

Ainsley couldn't leave him. Not like this. She'd never live that down.

Sighing, she turned and went back towards the house.

———

A minute later, she was back inside the kitchen, and a minute after that, she was in the second-floor hallway, her ear pressed against a closed door.

"I got you," she said.

This lock was easy. From the outside, it had a simple deadbolt. Ainsley flipped it and then turned the doorknob. The door swung open.

Brian stood there, wrists ziptied like her, but he had a small bloody injury on the side of his head.

"What did they do to you?"

"I resisted," he said.

"My God, I'm so sorry—"

She went to touch it, but he flinched. "We'll do it later. How did you get out of your room?"

Ainsley explained it to him.

"I knew I liked the cut of your style," he said. "It wouldn't have worked on this door."

"You got the heavy-duty room," she said. "They probably thought the woman wouldn't try to escape, so they gave me the workers' nap room."

"What kind of organization is this?" he said.

"You know the answer to that," she replied. "Come on, let's go."

As they descended the staircase, the sound of a car engine approached. Ainsley peered outside. Through the living room window, she could see an SUV arriving, the same one that had driven them here.

"Oh man," said Brian, "shit shit shit—"

They descended to the main room. Ainsley made a quick decision. There wasn't enough time to get out of the house. They'd have to hide.

Where?

A small door near the kitchen silently called her name. That was a basement. She went over to it, yanked on the knob. It came off in her hand.

"What the—"

"I got this," said Brian.

He stuck his fingers into the hole that was left by the knob and gently worked it. The door popped open.

"Get in there," he said.

Ainsley descended into the pitch darkness, dragging her hands along the wall in a champion's gesture, trying to balance herself. Brian followed her, carefully closing the door behind him.

———

They paused on the narrow stairs. It smelled like damp rot in the cellar. She heard the scurrying of unseen rats.

"I really don't want to go any further," she whispered.

"We have to," he said.

She fumbled in her bag for her phone. She opened it and turned on the flashlight and swept it across the cellar. Piles of junk. Undefinable heaps of decay. The wet dog smell of mold and mildew. Invisible spores of fungi floated through the air and into her nose. Ainsley sneezed silently into her sleeve.

She gingerly set foot on the floor of the basement. Brian was half a step behind her.

Upstairs, they heard the men arrive. She cut out the light. They stood there in the darkness, faces lifted to the ceiling, listening to the footsteps.

"The question is whether they come down here," whispered Brian.

"They will if they're thorough," she said. "Or they'll assume we're running down the street."

"So this could be the safest decision."

"Don't jinx it."

They heard the footsteps run up and down the upstairs staircase. Then they heard the voices talking. Finally they heard the kitchen door slam and the car start up again. It drove off.

"We can leave now," he whispered.

"We can't go upstairs. They might've left somebody this time."

"What do we do?"

Ainsley pulled out her phone again, swept the basement a second time. She stopped. On the far side of the basement was a short set of stairs, covered in decay. At the top of the stairs was a pair of small ancient double doors. They were made of wood, painted red, and angled slightly inward.

It was an old-fashioned cellar entrance, the type that people of the past used for delivering perishable goods directly into a basement. Here in Chicago, she guessed that it had been used to secretly store booze during Prohibition.

"We go out that way," she said. "Can you open it?"

Brian took a deep breath. "I can try."

With Ainsley holding the light, he picked his way across the basement, climbed the stairs, and studied the setup. "It's latched and locked. We can't open it."

"Can you break through?"

"I don't think so."

"You're a big guy."

Brian's face changed as he recognized his opportunity to impress Ainsley. He grew prouder. "Okay, fine."

He placed his shoulder against the old wood and pushed it gently. "This might not work. It's not as rotted as you would think."

"Wait, Brian." Ainsley looked around. On the floor she spotted a tool. It was a long flat blade, slightly curved.

"A pry bar," she said. She picked it up. "Use this."

"What are the odds?" he said, examining it.

"That they would have one? Pretty good. These are criminals."

Brian jammed the pry bar into the seam between the two doors. He began working it, left and right, jimmying it.

Then he gave a tremendous shove, and the doors broke open.

"Let's go!" he said.

He dropped the pry bar. Ainsley picked it up again.

He burst out into the sunlight, Ainsley right behind him. She heard a voice shouting.

They were already fully in the elongated space between the side of the house and the fence. Brian and Ainsley shuffled quickly down the narrow path towards the front yard. Passing the corner of the house, they crossed the yard towards the sedan when Ainsley sensed a movement to her left.

On the opposite corner of the house, Ratface had just appeared and was turning his gun towards them.

"Down!" she shouted to Brian.

He fired just as she and Brian dove to the ground behind the car parked on the lawn. The mouth of the pistol barked.

"He's coming around!" said Brian.

Ainsley's fingers gripped the pry bar. Rising to her feet, she cocked her arms back and flung the bar towards the assailant. It spun like a helicopter blade in the air.

She only had one opportunity, and it was a perfect throw. The criminal was swinging his pistol around at the same moment the pry bar connected with his ratface. He went down like a bag of topsoil.

Brian rose quickly, ran over, and placed one boot on his forearm, his other boot on the man's neck.

"Grab the weapon!" he said.

Ainsley ran over, keeping clear of the muzzle of the gun, and unpeeled it from his hand.

Recovering himself, Ratface began to struggle. Brian gave the man a swift kick in the head. He stopped moving.

"Now," he said, "we run like hell."

"I don't want to carry a gun!" said Ainsley.

"Then give it to me. We could need it in this neighborhood."

"Where are we?"

He scanned the horizon. The Chicago skyline loomed large on the skyline, larger than it had been in Uptown, or near the futsal facility. "I'd say Pilsen. Mexican town."

That was all Ainsley needed to hear.

"So they're cartel," she said.

It was the first time she'd said it out loud. She hadn't dared to voice the thought until now. The implications were too vast.

Brian didn't respond right away. Then he said, "Are you ready?"

"Yes."

They took off at a brisk walk down the street, both hands ziptied. They approach a main road, with traffic. Family strolled along. Taxis zipped by.

"Can you get rid of that thing now?" Ainsley said.

Brian gently placed the pistol into someone's trash can and closed the lid.

"Happy?"

"I'll be happy once we're far away from here."

On the main street, Ainsley held her bag and coat over her ziptied hands. It looked like she was trying to maintain her modesty.

Brian hailed a passing taxi. They climbed in and shut the door. As the car carried them out of the neighborhood, leaving the trap house and the criminals far behind her, Ainsley exhaled.

"Well, I'm glad I could protect you so well," Brian cracked.

She maintained the sarcasm. "Yeah, I really owe you for that."

"Then come out with me on Friday."

He was looking at her with earnest eyes, but Ainsley shook her head sadly. "I'm leaving this city, Brian. I'm going home."

CHAPTER THIRTY-ONE

Three days later, Ainsley sat inside her car, parked on the street outside of her apartment complex. From here, she could see her own front door.

She was trying to build up the nerve to go back inside.

Ainsley had left Chicago as soon as was humanly possible. By four o'clock that same day as her kidnapping and escape, she'd been on a short flight home.

Arriving back in her hometown that evening, she'd been too frightened to go back home. So she'd checked into a basic hotel near the airport and flopped on the bed and looked at her phone.

No calls from Jared. No calls from Wayne. No calls from Deirdre.

No calls from anybody at all.

She was a woman without context. She knew people, of course, but increasingly it felt as though they didn't know her.

For the next two days, Ainsley had sat in a booth in the hotel lobby, eating miserable breakfasts from the six-thirty-to-ten-am buffet. A styrofoam bowl of corn flakes. A mini blueberry muffin. A spatula's worth of scrambled eggs. All with flimsy plasticware wrapped inside of even more plastic.

This was the real American experience.

Each day she'd passed by her apartment, frightened to slow down. Each time, she'd imagined assassins parked inside anonymous black vehicles, watching her front door like murderous hawks. She'd done this even when the only vehicle on the street was an empty fifteen-year-old Datsun with rust spots and two flat tires.

Ainsley knew she was probably being ridiculous. But she also wanted to play it very, very cautious. The boss had said Jared's name.

Now, however, she'd judged that the time was right. She was hundreds of miles from Chicago, and several days had passed.

She took a deep breath, then shut off her engine. She opened the car door, exited, shut the door.

Ainsley marched up the sidewalk towards her own front door. In her right hand were her house keys. In her left hand was a small canister of pepper spray, the cap unlocked and ready.

She peered in the window. It was dark inside. From what she could make out, nothing had changed.

Ainsley went over to the front door. She unlocked the deadbolt, then turned the key in the doorknob. The door swung open.

She leapt aside, flattening herself against the side of the exterior wall. Just in case a man came barging out with semi-automatic weaponry blazing.

But nobody came outside. Ainsley calmed herself down and entered her own home.

In the living room, she turned on the overhead light fixture, the one she'd never liked. The room was exactly the way she'd left it: sofa, television, bookshelf, even the remote control and the receipts on the coffee table.

Then she went into the bedroom. It was the same. The blankets on the bed were undisturbed, and her sweater was right where she'd left it on the floor.

In the kitchen, Ainsley flicked on the light—and that's when she saw it.

On the kitchen table was a small jewelry box, a cheap flip phone, and a note.

On the note were two words in a very familiar handwriting. *Call me.*

As she reached for the box, Ainsley felt it suddenly hard to breathe. Her trembling fingers fumbled for the crack. Finding it, they cracked the box open.

Inside lay her engagement ring.

————

Ainsley withdrew the ring from the box and held it up to the light.

That was her engagement ring, no doubt. She knew it better than any other piece of jewelry in her collection, for obvious reasons. The two-point-one carat diamond, as clear as Caribbean water. The scalloped pave setting. The stamped dimples around the gold band.

This was it.

Ainsley started to slip it on her finger, then quickly pulled it off. No, she wouldn't be wearing it again. That wasn't the point of this.

The point had been to find and retain control of the one thing in this whole miserable stinking marriage that continued to mean something to her.

But she *hadn't* found it. Someone else had.

Ainsley picked up the cell phone and dialed her ex-husband's number. It rang once, twice, then went to voice-mail. She disconnected without leaving a message.

He hadn't picked up. She stared at the small flip phone, annoyed.

A moment later, the phone's display lit up. It was a number she didn't recognize.

Chewing on her lip, she decided to take the leap. She flipped the phone open and held it up to her ear.

"Hello," she said.

"Ainsley," said the voice.

It was him.

Her husband, or rather her soon-to-be ex-husband, the Legal Weasel. Birth name: Jared Walker.

"What the hell, Jared," she said.

"Yeah—"

"I don't even know where to begin—"

"Well, I'm not apologizing," he said.

"You owe me some kind of explanation—"

"And I'm not explaining either—"

"I am your wife," she spat, "and you can't just disappear on your legally wedded spouse, with no rhyme or reason, no accountability—"

"Of course I can," he said. "I already did."

"You are such an asshole."

"You're right. I'm a prick."

"What?"

"I'm agreeing with you, Ainsley. I treated you badly and I walked out in an even worse way."

"If I'd known four years ago what I know now—"

He sighed. "Trust me, it was better this way. There's a lot you don't know."

"Obviously."

"Look, you've got the ring again. You deserve it. I shouldn't have taken it from you."

"Aren't you going to ask what I was doing?"

"I know what you were doing."

"How?"

"Because I know."

"You won't even explain that?"

He sighed. "Look on the inside lining of your white bag."

Ainsley felt a wave of panic rising inside her body. She ran over to her bag, which she'd flung on the sofa.

"Look for a slit in the inside lining."

Her fingers found a slit. She hadn't even noticed it.

"Now slip one finger inside. What do you feel?"

She obeyed. There was a small disk, no bigger than the tip of her finger.

"It feels like a button."

"It's a tracker."

White-hot pangs of anger stabbed Ainsley in the head, the neck, the shoulders, the back. She wanted to fling the phone across the room. The Legal Weasel been tracking her this entire time—from Miami to California to Vegas to Chicago. He'd pinpointed her location at every waking moment, all because he'd known how much she valued that white bag, and how she carried it around everywhere she went.

"Goddamn you," she said. "You knew everything."

"Well, I knew your location. Just like you knew mine, Ainsley."

She fell silent, waiting for him to ask how she'd managed to track him too. But he didn't. She was grateful for that, because she never would've wanted to throw Wayne under the bus.

"Why did you give that ring to that kid at Trebuchet

winery? Fernando? You didn't leave it by accident. You gave it to him."

"That's one of things I can't tell you."

"You knew he was going to Chicago. You knew the people he was mixed up with."

The other end of the line fell silent once again.

She drew a breath and asked the big question: "Are you involved with the Mexican cartels?"

"No," he said.

"That's a lie," she retorted. "That's your first lie."

"Look—"

"The man who kidnapped me in Chicago said your name, Jared! He said it!"

"Well, I honestly don't know how that happened—"

"Yes, you do, you weasel—"

"Look, it would be better if you didn't know anything about—"

"Answer me this—and tell me the damn truth. Are you laundering money for a transnational organized criminal syndicate?"

He paused. Then: "No."

Ainsley's breath out of her nose came in angry short spurts, like from a bull's nostrils. She was certain he'd just lied again, but she didn't have proof.

"If what you're doing is legal," she replied, "you wouldn't have any problem telling me."

"Maybe I don't want you to know!" he said, raising his voice. "Maybe I just want you out of my life, Ainsley!"

"Maybe I want you out of mine!" she shouted back.

"Fine!"

"Fine!"

They both stopped. This was the ultimate moment of truth.

He was the first to break. "I was waiting for you to do

something wrong, so I'd have a reason to leave you. But you never did. So I left anyways."

Against her wishes, Ainsley felt her heart soften. She'd been carrying guilt about her role in the end of her marriage. She'd doubted herself as a spouse, as a woman, as a human. He'd just dispelled those doubts.

"Do you want me to say thank you?" she said.

"Say whatever you want. You've got your ring, you've got your life, and you've got your divorce as soon as you get the paperwork to my attorney. I'll send you his address tomorrow."

"But—"

"Tell me how much it costs, and we'll split it."

"But—"

"Do you have any other questions?"

Ainsley fought the urge to ask the weakest question possible, the one that would lay bare the vulnerability that she felt inside her own heart. But the other, wiser part of her spoke up. His response didn't matter.

"No," she said.

"Okay. Take care, Ainsley."

"You too."

They disconnected.

Whatever her ex-husband had once felt for her, Ainsley was positive that he didn't love her anymore.

CHAPTER THIRTY-TWO

Hours later, Ainsley sat at the edge of a bonfire, staring at the ring.

Why was she still holding onto it? It represented a massive crash-and-burn, a pair of lives lived in parallel until one line had turned perpendicular. Why didn't she sell it? After all, the price of gold had skyrocketed. Somebody would give her several hundred dollars for it. She sure needed the money.

Ainsley looked at her watch. It read six thirty. She could leave now, make it to the jewelry district by seven. She knew that a handful of shops stayed open in the evening to cater to the admittedly thinner nighttime jewelry crowds.

In a flash, she was on her feet. The ring was stowed in her pocket, the fire still burning low.

Keys jangling in her hand, Ainsley stumbled away from the pit towards her car.

Half an hour later, Ainsley was cruising through the heart of the jewelry district. She found a parking spot on the street and leaped out.

The sun had dropped behind the buildings. Automatic streetlamps were buzzing on. People scurried by, either on their way home to dinner or on their way out to the bars.

Ainsley leaned against a parking meter, scanning the block. Jake's Jewelry was closed. So was the watch repair shop owned by the stubbly Armenian who always tried to hit on her. Across the street, the massive Gemstone Cooperative had already rolled down its metal shutters.

She strode quickly to the next block. More store signs blinking off. She watched an Open sign flip to Closed. Silent street characters glided past like monks, the small white earbuds playing secret hymns into their ears.

She tried a few more blocks, but no luck. It seemed that every jewelry store in the district had closed at the same minute. Ainsley felt frustrated. She didn't want to return here another day. She wanted to sell the ring *now*, to purge herself of this ridiculous husband *now*, to change her life *now*.

Then she passed the opening to a narrow brick alley. At the end of the alley was a small neon light. In the shape of a diamond.

A jewelry shop. And it was open.

Ainsley chewed on her lip. She'd always avoided this place. Deirdre had jokingly called it Rape Lane. In fact, this scenario had all the makings of disaster: drunk woman, diamond ring, neon lights, seedy alley.

But her life already had become a slow-moving disaster. Why the hell not?

She felt around inside her purse until she found the small canister of pepper spray. She unlocked the pin.

The long walk felt more treacherous than it had seemed. Overflowing trash bins, flattened cardboard boxes, broken rain gutters. A homeless man lifted an arm towards her and groaned.

She ran the last few steps, then ducked her head as she entered the store.

———

The shop was the size of her bedroom and smelled like sesame oil. An elderly Asian man sat at his small desk slurping a bowl of noodles and reading a foreign newspaper. The only jewelry on display was under the glass case between them.

She cleared her throat. The man didn't look up.

"Do you buy diamond rings here?" she said.

The shop owner kept his nose in the paper. He was either deaf or antisocial. Ainsley slapped the engagement ring on the glass counter. It made a hard crack. The shop owner looked up.

"Yes?"

"I want to sell this."

He laid down his chopsticks across the bowl and wiped his hands. He approached the counter, lifted the ring, and analyzed it, pursing his lips. Then he laid it on a small scale.

"Only this?"

"Yes."

"I can give you five hundred dollars cash. Or eight hundred in store credit."

"It's worth more than that."

He shrugged. She glanced down into the case. It offered the usual array of gaudy hearts, crucifixes, smiley faces—all decorated with citrine, blue topaz, smoky topaz, quartzite.

Then one ring caught her eye. It featured a cabochon cut turquoise.

"That one's pretty."

"Yes, very lovely." The man drummed his fingers on the glass. "If you like that, I will show you something even better."

He turned to a safe, spun the dial, then opened the door. Inside were several rows of trays. He slid out the lowest one and brought it over.

On the tray was a silver squash-blossom necklace.

Ainsley felt her heart flutter. She'd always had a soft spot for Native American jewelry. She'd studied it, fingered it, modeled it, adored it, emailed craftsmen about it, dreamed about it. A beautiful piece of handcrafted silver-and-turquoise jewelry was something to behold.

This piece in particular was a Navajo classic. It boasted ten beautiful little squash blossoms on each side of the *naja*, or crescent-shaped pendant, that hung in the middle. Ainsley had salivated over similar necklaces in the past, but had never bought one. Partly because of the cost, partly because they felt too ethnic, too proprietary to the native peoples who produced them.

Still, she admired the silverwork, imagining the pony-tailed artisan as he sweated over the soldering, the scribing, the chiseling, the filing.

"This is *fantastic*," she said. "Is it Cerillos turquoise or Stinich?"

The jeweler's wide eyes, magnified by his thick lenses, grew even wider.

"Ah—"

"Don't lie."

He shrugged. "Honestly, I don't know, I'm sorry. What is the difference?"

"Cerillos is from New Mexico," she said, "while Stinich is from Nevada."

He shifted uneasily. "I can find out and let you know."

Ainsley felt frustrated. She wasn't supposed to be giving

jewelry lessons to a jeweler. And she wasn't trying to stump him to get an ego boost either. She was honestly curious.

"Don't worry about it," she said. "What are you asking?"

The jeweler's eyes fixed hers, totally unreadable. "Eight hundred."

Ainsley cocked an eyebrow. Why so low? Maybe he'd done a nosedive just for her. To see if she'd bite.

In the meantime, she had lifted the necklace. It felt cold and heavy, like a chain, in her fingers. She turned it over, inspecting all the crevices. And then she noticed something.

A date.

On the back of one of the squash blossoms were four tiny numbers: 1892.

Ainsley immediately recognized their significance. The necklace had been made out of coin silver, as opposed to ingot silver. In nineteenth-century America, the Zunis had taken every opportunity to melt the white man's currency into jewelry. And, occasionally, bits of the coins survived.

Those four small numerals tripled its value.

At least.

CHAPTER THIRTY-THREE

Ainsley's heart thumped in her chest. This back-alley jeweler had no idea of the value of the squash-blossom necklace. Maybe he was new to the gem business. Maybe he was subbing for the real owner. Maybe he only knew how to sell gaudy rings to total newbs and was in over his head with this piece.

The problem was that Ainsley didn't have eight hundred dollars. She couldn't even think of a way to *get* eight hundred dollars. But she could trade the ring for it. He'd said he would give eight hundred dollars in store credit.

She could then flip the necklace to another jeweler, and at least double or maybe triple her investment.

This had to be done. For herself, and for the good of all jewelry everywhere.

"Let's do it," she said. "Even trade. My ring for your necklace."

A queer smile came across the jeweler's face. He closed the case on the squash-blossom necklace and, to Ainsley's surprise, returned it to the vault. Then he closed and locked the door.

"What are you doing?" she said. "I want to buy that."

"I know."

"Why are you putting it away?"

"It was coin silver," he said. "I could sell it for three thousand dollars."

Her mouth dropped open. This sneaky bastard had known its real value all along.

"Then why—"

"It was a test," he said. "Here is your money for the ring."

The jeweler pulled five hundred dollars from the cash register and placed it on the glass between them. He kept his fingers on one half of the money. When Ainsley reached for it, he pulled it away quickly.

"I hate games," she said.

"Before you leave, I want to make you an offer. But I need to ask you a question first."

"Sure, why not."

"What was your favorite subject in school?"

This was out of left field. Ainsley didn't have a head for math. She still sometimes counted on her fingers, which didn't embarrass her in the least, and she possessed only slightly more interest in science. But she had always loved reading literature and history, and most of all she'd loved learning foreign languages. They came easy to her. That was her one gift.

"Foreign languages," she said.

The jeweler betrayed a smile. He went to the back of the office, which was about four steps away. Found a soft black leather case and unzipped it carefully. He returned to the counter with a single business card. He placed it on top of the five hundred dollars and slid both towards Ainsley.

"Please call this number. Tell them that I referred you." He paused. "You can make much more money there than you will by flipping that necklace."

Ainsley read the card. There were two words, *Associated Industries*, followed by a phone number. She'd never seen a blander business card in her life.

"Why?" she said.

"They are looking for a person like you."

Ainsley was hesitant. "I don't think I'm interested."

He took her hand. "This could be the best thing that ever happened to you. Please take it."

The Asian man was looking at her intently. Something about his manner made Ainsley realize that he wasn't messing with her. This felt like it was for real.

"Thank you for the information," she said.

"Make sure you say my name, Elmer Yang. Here." He wrote it on the back. "And what is your name?"

"Ainsley."

"I will let them know to expect your phone call, Miss Ainsley."

She looked at the card. "What kind of place is this?"

"You will find out when you go. I can't say anything more."

Mystified, Ainsley pocketed the five hundred dollars and the business card and left the shop. She glanced back and saw him watching her. He made a telephone shape with his thumb and pinky finger.

CHAPTER THIRTY-FOUR

The conversation had been quick. The woman who'd answered the phone at Associated Industries had said her name was Martina. The jeweler had called her about Ainsley. She'd declined to discuss her business over the phone.

But she'd agreed to meet the next day.

Now Ainsley had arrived ten minutes early at the given address. It was an ordinary suburban office complex. Every day across America, millions of businesspeople went to work in such structures.

She adjusted her makeup in the rearview mirror, reapplied her lipstick. Everything looked good. She closed her compact, left the car, slammed the door shut with her hip, then remembered to brush off her skirt.

She strode across the parking lot towards the door. The asphalt seemed hard, clear, and profound. She felt a sense of purpose.

Ainsley pressed the buzzer. A heavy beep sounded inside. She waited. The air felt weird and hazy. She felt like she was entering the wardrobe in the famous children's story.

A petite woman in her sixties answered the door. She

wore a simple gray pantsuit: a work outfit, somewhat formal. Her black hair was swept into a stiff updo, held together with bobby pins.

She held her chin stiffly as her eyes swept up and down her guest.

Ainsley cleared her throat. "Martina? I'm Ainsley Walker. I'm supposed to tell you that Elmer recommended me."

She offered her hand, but the woman didn't take it.

She merely said, "I know."

Martina appeared to be white, but her voice sported a soft Latin accent. It sounded unlike anything Ainsley had ever heard before. And now she was standing there, one arm stiff against the door, sizing up her visitor the way an art dealer might appraise a potential purchase.

"Do you have another job?" the woman said.

"No."

"Do you have children?"

"No."

Then she squinted. She was looking at Ainsley's bracelet. It was composed of links of bezel-set amethyst. This was one of her most eye-catching pieces, which is precisely why she'd worn it.

"*Amatista*," said the woman.

"It's one of my favorites."

"You prefer the vintage style?"

"Who doesn't?"

She smiled. "Do you have a passport?"

Now it was Ainsley's turn to smile, because those were magic words, ones that would win her heart.

"Of course."

"Do you have any Spanish?"

"I have enough. *A dónde quiere enviarme?*" In other words: *Where do you want to send me?*

"Please come in," said Martina. "We can have a discussion,

and then maybe you will find out." She moved aside, gesturing for her visitor to enter.

Drawing a deep breath, Ainsley Walker stepped inside.

PLOTWORKS PUBLISHING

If you enjoyed this story, please leave a review at the place where you purchased it.

Then visit Plotworks Publishing to follow Ainsley Walker on her next exciting gemstone travel mystery!

Now turn the page for a sneak peek—

THE URUGUAY AMETHYST

AN AINSLEY WALKER
GEMSTONE TRAVEL MYSTERY

J.A. JERNAY

THE URUGUAY AMETHYST

The Uruguay Amethyst

Ainsley pulled the backseat door closed. Her driver's eyes looked at her in the rearview mirror.

"Where can I take you?" Oswaldo asked in Spanish.

"Back to Tabarez," she said.

He nodded, and they pulled away from the curb. Ainsley studied him in the mirror. His jaw was set firmly. She decided to see what she could learn from him.

"Do you like working for Tabarez?" she said.

"Yes," he said. Nothing else.

Of course he wouldn't comment on his employer. She decided to stick to facts.

"Oswaldo, after lunch I will need you to help me take a very large package to this address." She handed him the paper with Bernabé's address. "Can you find this place?"

He read the address and nodded. Not a word. Ainsley was beginning to wonder if he was a bit simple.

The car was slicing down La Rambla, and Ainsley contented herself with staring out the window, at the blurring breakwall and at the choppy brown water of the delta. The sky was bright blue and the clouds puffy and white and a chill wind was blowing again.

It was mesmerizing. She wrapped her coat around herself more tightly and snuggled in.

Then she woke up to Oswaldo touching her knee. The vehicle had stopped. She was outside Tabarez's house.

Ainsley emerged from the vehicle and buttoned the top collar of her coat. "It's so cold here," she said.

Oswaldo didn't respond. Conversationally, there was no difference between her driver and a piece of drywall. She decided to just issue him orders instead. It would save both of them a lot of trouble.

"Stay here until I return."

He lit a cigarette and looked straight ahead.

Slinging her purse over her shoulder, Ainsley walked alone towards the house. Her stomach was twisting itself into anxious knots. Partly because of El Árbol Negro, partly because she was so hungry.

And nervous. She was about to enjoy homemade ñoquis in a private dining room with an extremely wealthy and attractive man who may or may not have refused to sleep with her, even after she'd thrown herself at him. Why did she have to black out on that night of all nights? And now he was going to sell her a famous amethyst after telling her its secret history.

This felt too good to be true.

The copper gate was rolled wide open. Ainsley cocked her head. That was strange, given the value of the contents inside the mansion.

She stepped through the open gate onto the driveway, then moved into the manicured yard. It made her heart sing again. She touched the bougainvillea, listened to the branches clacking in the breeze from the estuary.

Then she rang the front doorbell and waited. The slab of wood before her was exquisite. Spirals and whorls had been dug into its surface, like the enormous thumbprint of a criminal.

There was no response. That was weird. Heinrik was the epitome of the efficient manservant. He should've been there in a flash.

She rang the doorbell again, then turned and surveyed the landscaping. Water was trickling from some unseen fountain. She couldn't find it. An invisible bird sang crookedly from the branches of a tall ash. She couldn't find that either. A sinking feeling filled her stomach.

Had she been lied to? Had Tabarez cast her aside that quickly? Had he decided to keep El Árbol Negro? She'd heard the old cliché of how Latin people lived for the moment, but this expulsion was quicker than she'd expected. She felt anger sprouting from her back like a bouquet of hot orange flames.

Upset, she turned back to the door. If he wouldn't answer the door, she would invite herself inside. She gripped the doorknob and turned it. The slab of wood swung open easily, as though it weighed ten pounds instead of twenty times that much. Of course Tabarez had made sure that the hinges were well-oiled.

She entered the foyer and noticed a large object, wrapped in black plastic, resting immediately next to the door.

El Árbol Negro.

With her fingertips she traced its lovely branches beneath the plastic. So beautiful. She noticed a dolly sitting next to it. How thoughtful.

Remembering her host's orders, she kicked off her shoes, then crept around the edges of the carpet. The house was completely silent.

"José Ignacio?" she shouted. "Heinrik?"

Still no response. She crept up the stairs to the second

floor sitting room where she had last seen him, in his white robe, strumming his instrument.

As she rose to the landing, she caught her breath.

José Ignacio was still sitting on the sofa in the sumptuous second floor sala. The guitar was laying next to him. His head was tilted back, and his eyes were shut. A thin smile decorated his mouth.

Another thin smile, this one quite a bit redder, and eight inches across, decorated his throat.

José Ignacio Tabarez was not going to be dining with her this afternoon.

He was dead.

PLOTWORKS PUBLISHING

Visit Plotworks Publishing to follow Ainsley Walker on her next exciting gemstone travel mystery!

Then explore a different series by J.A. Jernay—the Cosmo Bennett Mapping Thrillers!

Turn the page for a sneak peek—

J.A. JERNAY

BOUNDARY

A
COSMO
BENNETT
MAPPING
THRILLER

FROM *THE AUTHOR OF THE AINSLEY WALKER*
GEMSTONE TRAVEL MYSTERY SERIES

BOUNDARY

Cosmo and his assistant Noah shuffled down the dirt shoulder of the boulevard in the midday heat, sweating and miserable.

Each was lost in his own thoughts. Cosmo dreamed of hitting a heavy punching bag at his gymnasium. Noah dreamed of passing level nineteen of Operation Earlobe, an obscure RPG he'd abandoned last semester.

The morning's meeting had been a complete bust.

"I don't think we should continue," said Cosmo finally.

Noah didn't respond, but Cosmo took no notice. He continued: "I don't think anybody here takes our task seriously. I don't think this propaganda map was as influential as they say. I don't think this map has driven the civil unrest. I think social media and centuries of tribal warfare are more to blame for the unrest than anything else."

He looked over at Noah, waiting for a response. "What about you?"

The graduate assistant came back from his reverie. "Huh?"

"Did you hear anything I said?"

"No."

"I was just saying this is pointless and we should go home."

"I don't have a problem with that."

They arrived at Vida e Caffe. It was a chain café, with hundreds of similar franchises scattered across the southern part of the African continent. The branding was modern and inviting. A hundred people sat beneath umbrellas at small tables on the large outdoor patio.

An arm was waving at them. It was Christopher, their fixer, a cup of tea on a ceramic saucer in front of him. Two other cups awaited them.

"Hello sirs," he said. "I ordered us all a rooibos. It's a vanilla tea that is extraordinary."

Cosmo and Noah pulled out the chairs and sat down. The driver quickly sussed out that something was wrong.

"It was a bad meeting?" he said quietly.

"Yes," said Cosmo, "there was no progress made."

"I'm very sorry."

Cosmo sighed. "I think we have to leave."

The fixer looked confused. "But you just sat down—"

"The country," he clarified. "We have to leave Fabajouti. We can't seem to do any good here."

Christopher looked crestfallen. "I do understand your frustration."

Noah said, "If it's okay with you, we'd probably like to just get in the car and go back to the hotel."

The fixer rediscovered his manners. "Of course, as you wish—"

"But we'd love to try the tea first—" added Cosmo.

"You two enjoy the rooibos," said Christopher, "while I fetch the car. The parking lot is very jammed and it will take quite a while to remove. I've already paid the bill."

Before they could object, the driver had shot to his feet.

He clapped Cosmo on the shoulder and left the patio. They watched him cross the boulevard to an off-street parking area that was crammed tightly with vehicles. On his approach, the attendant began shifting other vehicles.

Noah sipped the tea. "This does taste really good. I don't drink enough tea."

"I like tea," said Cosmo. He sipped from the cup. "This one is good."

"What's your favorite?" asked Noah.

"Maybe pu'er."

"That one's bitter, right?"

"Yeah. It's fermented."

"What about Earl Grey?"

"A cliché."

"I think I'm more of a fruity tea guy," said Noah.

Cosmo nodded. "Yeah, they have their charms."

"You ever try chamomile?"

"It's good for sleeping," said Cosmo, "but otherwise it's—"

His comment was cut short by a massive fireball that erupted from the parking lot across the street.

———

In a split second, Cosmo and Noah instinctively rolled off their chairs and onto the ground beneath their table. Their eyes met. Each was filled with terror.

Then the shock of the overpressure hit. Cosmo felt the force of the blast wave hit the left side of his body. The highly compressed air rattled the left side of his skull. It even sent his lips and cheeks flapping to the right.

The initial sound of the explosion was deafening, but that was soon replaced by a symphony of falling destruction. A thousand pieces of metal, plastic, glass, and upholstery rained down upon the boulevard, the grass, the other cars.

A shower of tiny shrapnel hit on the patio of the cafe. One hit Noah in the hand and sizzled his flesh. He shook it off.

They waited another few seconds for the shrapnel rain to end. Then Cosmo and Noah lifted their heads.

The patio of the café was transformed into pandemonium. The patrons started to pull themselves up from the ground and flee out to the street and in the opposite direction. The street itself was coming alive with panicked people running in every direction.

"What the actual—" said Noah.

"Christopher!" interrupted Cosmo. "What about Christopher?"

He scrambled up to his feet. Without waiting for Noah, he sprinted out of the café and across the boulevard, weaving through the stopped cars. The air was acrid with chemicals and the heat had somehow intensified even further.

The parking lot was a field of wreckage. The bomb had exploded in the middle of the space, shredding every vehicle and person within twenty meters. Pieces of concrete and metal and glass had been blown across the scene.

"Christopher!" he shouted again. "Christopher! Don't do this!"

He saw a shoe with a foot still in it. He saw a red string of guts entangled in a hubcap. A wave of nausea gripped his stomach. He covered his nose with his t-shirt and backed away.

He tripped backwards over a piece of metal, stumbled, and fell to the ground.

That's when he saw it.

A long strip of shredded fabric. A yellow-and-green printed tropical shirt.

It was bloody and torn.

Cosmo turned his head and retched onto the asphalt. All the tea he'd just drank came out.

He somehow pulled himself to his feet and staggered back to the café. Noah was waiting at the far corner, on the sidewalk, pacing frantically.

"So?"

"I found him," said Cosmo. He forced the next words out. "A little bit."

Noah's face went white. "Oh my God."

Cosmo didn't say anything. He just gripped Noah by the upper arm. "Walk with me. And don't look back."

———

The pair moved briskly down the boulevard, away from the scene. People were running past them, mouths open, eyes full of fear, but Cosmo maintained a steady pace. His face betrayed an intense desire to appear as normal as possible.

"So we're just going to leave the scene?" said Noah.

"Yep."

"Why?"

"Don't make me answer that, Noah."

"I think we should talk to the police, cooperate, tell them everything—"

"In a different country," Cosmo replied, "in a different scenario, you'd be right. But not here, not now."

Noah looked back over his shoulder at the scene.

"Look straight ahead," Cosmo said through his teeth, "and listen to me. Our Mercedes is gone. Christopher is ... gone."

"Shit—"

"And I'm going to suggest something else that could blow your mind."

"What?"

"It's possible that we were the intended target."

"That's insane."

"Is it?"

"How do you know?"

"I don't. But it's a possibility. Here's another one. It's possible that we are going to be used as scapegoats. We were the last people seen eating with Christopher. Do you want to be put in a Fabajouti jail on suspicion of a crime?"

They walked for another half minute in silence. Behind them, the chaos grew distant.

"Where are we going?" Noah said finally.

"Back to the hotel."

"And then?"

"We're leaving, like we planned."

"We're not going home, are we?" said Noah.

Cosmo's mouth grew hard and his jaw jutted out. He stared straight forward at an invisible point on the horizon. "No, we're not."

PLOTWORKS PUBLISHING

Visit Plotworks Publishing today for all these titles—and more!